As Dev got closer to the desk, several members of the group parted, revealing the man at the center of their orbit, his toned physique filling out a set of faded blue scrubs to perfection.

His back was to Dev, so he couldn't see the man's face, but based on the tingling in his bloodstream, he didn't need to. It was the tawny hair and wide, confident stance that did it. He'd recognize those anywhere.

Guess that answered his question.

Dammit. He did not need this today.

Dev stopped where he was and turned away fast, but not fast enough, apparently.

"Is that you, Dev?" Val said from behind him, a touch of the same astonishment in his voice that Dev felt inside at seeing his old friend again. "I'd heard you were back in town, but didn't know you were starting here today."

Throat tight, Dev took a deep breath and turned slowly. Best get it over with now. He gave Val a curt nod, taking refuge behind his professional façade. "Dr. Laurent."

Dear Reader,

I'm so happy to finally bring my first male-male romance to the Harlequin Medical Romance line. This story has been a long time coming for me, going through many iterations with my editors until we settled on the perfect story at last. I've been an avid fan, reader and writer of LGBTQA+ romance under a pen name and have always tried to include diversity and queer characters in all my Medical Romance stories up to this point as secondary characters. That's the world I live in and the world I want to continue to see for the future—where love is love and everyone is treated equally and with respect. But this book is the first time I've been given the green light to make my two amazing heroes front and center. I loved writing Dev and Val's second-chance journey from grief, fear and hurt to comfort, wholeness and happily-ever-after, with Val's adorable, Lego-loving son, Cam, along for the ride. I hope you fall in love with and enjoy this trio as much as I did in *A Single Dad to Heal Him*. Until next time...

Happy reading!

Traci <3

A SINGLE DAD TO HEAL HIM

TRACI DOUGLASS

MEDICAL ROMANCE

Harlequin®
MEDICAL ROMANCE

Recycling programs for this product may not exist in your area.

ISBN-13: 978-1-335-94300-2

A Single Dad to Heal Him

Copyright © 2025 by Traci Douglass

Harlequin Enterprises ULC
22 Adelaide St. West, 41st Floor
Toronto, Ontario M5H 4E3, Canada
www.Harlequin.com

Printed in U.S.A.

Traci Douglass is a *USA TODAY* bestselling romance author with Harlequin, Entangled Publishing and Tule Publishing, and has an MFA in writing popular fiction from Seton Hill University. She writes sometimes funny, usually awkward, always emotional stories about strong, quirky, wounded characters overcoming past adversity to find their forever person and heartfelt, healing happily-ever-afters. Connect with her through her website, tracidouglassbooks.com.

Books by Traci Douglass

Harlequin Medical Romance

Boston Christmas Miracles

Home Alone with the Children's Doctor

Wyckford General Hospital

Single Dad's Unexpected Reunion
An ER Nurse to Redeem Him
Her Forbidden Firefighter
Family of Three Under the Tree

Costa Rican Fling with the Doc
Island Reunion with the Single Dad
Their Barcelona Baby Bombshell
A Mistletoe Kiss in Manhattan
The GP's Royal Secret

Visit the Author Profile page
at Harlequin.com for more titles.

For all the misfits. For all those who are afraid to be who they are meant to be. For everyone scared to tell their truth. I see you. I feel you. I support you. I love you. Just as you are <3

CHAPTER ONE

I can't believe I'm back here again.

Dr. Devon Harrison's footsteps squeaked on the shiny linoleum floor as he walked down the corridor to Minneapolis Medical Center's emergency department, the heart of this busy teaching hospital. With each step, a sense of déjà vu coursed through him, bringing back memories of his time here as a resident, fresh out of the classroom and stupidly optimistic and trusting, ready to conquer the dreaded disease that was cancer, one tiny patient at a time.

He still wanted to cure as many kids as possible, but his ability to trust adults, especially when it came to himself, had shattered for good the year before and wasn't ever coming back. God, he still berated himself for being so naive. Why hadn't he seen the signs of betrayal, when looking back now they were so glaringly obvious? Well, he wouldn't make the same mistake again. He wouldn't trust his emotional instincts since they clearly didn't know what they were doing. Logic and reason and facts were his North Star in all things from here on out.

A set of automatic glass doors whooshed open in front of him, and he stepped into the controlled chaos of the ER. Nurses and techs bustled around, carrying equipment or tablets displaying digital charts, and orderlies wheeled patients around to their designated areas. The air vibrated with a constant low thrum of adrenaline—punctuated now and then with a pulse of urgency—tinged with the familiar scent of antiseptic. He'd been gone from this place for nearly a decade, completing his pediatric oncology fellowship in California where he'd moved with Tom—his now ex-husband—never imagining setting foot here again.

But life seemed to have a funny way of knocking you for a loop when you least expected it, at least it had in Dev's case. He stepped aside to allow a fast-moving gurney pushed by two paramedics to pass him, taking a moment to collect his thoughts. He'd been in town three weeks now since moving home while he waited on the final divorce papers and getting settled at his mother's house while he searched for a place of his own. His mother needed more help now since her MS was worsening and she was wheelchair bound, so it worked. Plus, staying busy helped distract him from the fact that other than his mother, he had no one now. Back in medical school he'd had a few close friends— well, one really close friend—but they'd lost touch after a falling-out before the wedding. A warning, really, about Tom that his friend had given him. A warning that Dev had been too besotted at the time to heed.

Boy, did he regret ignoring it now.

He wondered if Val was still around. Most of their class had scattered across the country after graduation, taking positions at different hospitals and medical centers or going into private practice, depending on their specialties. But the last he'd heard Val was still in Minneapolis. The last update Dev had gotten from his mother was after Val's sister's passing almost two years prior...

Dev honestly wasn't sure he wanted to see his old friend again. Not after everything that had happened. It would be beyond awkward, seeing the man who'd claimed Dev's fiancé had tried to sleep with him less than twenty-four hours before the wedding. Even now, Dev's gut tightened in response to that last fight with Val. He hadn't wanted to hear it, hadn't wanted to believe that the man he'd cast his usual caution aside for and gone all in on was not the person he'd thought he was. Back then, Dev had had too much time, too much emotion invested in the idealized future he'd planned with Tom to see the truth. So he'd gone through with the wedding and followed Tom to California, leaving Val and his accusations behind. He'd been wrong about Tom and Val had been right. Which Dev only interpreted as more proof that his own instincts and emotions were not to be trusted.

Better to keep to himself now. Safer that way. Even if it was a bit lonely.

With a sigh, Dev stared at a large whiteboard on the wall behind the nurses' station, scanning the information there to find the room his consult was in, but with so many people running around and scribbling orders everywhere, in the end the most expedient route was to just ask someone. He approached the central hub, noticing a small group of scrubs-clad staff gathered there, laughing and obviously friendly with each other. The kind of social group Dev had always yearned for growing up, but had never really figured out the knack of being part of one himself. Crowds tended to make him self-conscious and nervous, so he'd invariably close in on himself, making him appear aloof and unfriendly. But honestly, he was just painfully shy. Years of working with patients, and children in particular, had helped ease that social anxiety a bit, thankfully, but he still wasn't great at meeting new people. Especially now that he was on alert for possible deception everywhere he looked.

As Dev got closer to the desk, several members of the group parted, revealing the man at the center of their orbit, his toned physique filling out a set of faded blue scrubs to perfection. His back was to Dev, so he couldn't see the man's face, but based on the tingling in his bloodstream, he didn't need to. It was the tawny hair and wide, confident stance that did it. He'd recognized those details anywhere.

Guess that answered his question.

Dammit. He did not need this today.

Dev stopped where he was and turned away fast, but not fast enough, apparently.

"Is that you, Dev?" Val said from behind him, a touch of the same astonishment in his voice that Dev felt inside at seeing his old friend again. "I'd heard you were back in town, but didn't know you were starting here today."

Throat tight, Dev took a deep breath and turned slowly. Best get it over with now. He gave Val a curt nod, taking refuge behind his professional facade. "Dr. Laurent."

If Val was surprised by Dev's formality, he didn't show it, other than a slight quirk of one brow. Then again, Val always handled himself well in social situations. He'd been Mr. Popular during medical school. Everyone liked him. Given the coworkers flocking around him now, it seemed nothing had changed there since they'd last seen each other. Dev had never really understood how'd they'd ended up friends in the first place, other than maybe Val had felt sorry for him and taken him under his wing. And on paper, they did have a lot in common. They were both born and bred Minneapolitans, both queer, both determined to be the best physicians they could be and help as many people as possible along the way. But despite their different temperaments—or maybe because of them—as they'd spent more time together during marathon study sessions and brutally long residency hours, they'd become best friends. Val had been the closest person in the world to Dev back then. The one with whom he'd shared his deepest wishes and most outlandish dreams.

And for Dev, who'd always secretly blamed his own personal shortcomings for his own father leaving him and his mother behind when

Dev was five, having Val's friendship had felt like the sun coming out after a long, cloudy day. Dev had basked in that golden light, letting down his guard and opening himself up to new experiences, new emotions for the first time in his life. And maybe that's why he hadn't seen Tom coming. With the razzle-dazzle and potent sexiness of a rock star, Tom had swept Dev right off his feet and deftly dodged any concerns Dev might have had through sheer charisma. He'd invested fast and fully in the fantasy, thinking they'd live some kind of magical life together in southern California and any issues would vanish like a rabbit in a top hat. They were in love. What could possibly go wrong? And sure, deep down, Dev had inklings that maybe not everything was as it seemed with Tom. He'd seemed cagey about where he had gone when Dev couldn't get a hold of him. His stories of busy schedules and late-night meetings with his venture capital clients didn't always ring true. It was fine, Dev had told himself. He and Tom were in love and that meant they trusted each other. He was making problems out of nothing. He needed to lighten up, as Tom constantly reminded him. Dev was too uptight, too controlling, too suspicious. Just relax and go with the flow and everything would be just fine. Stop worrying. Then Val had come to him the night before the wedding saying Tom had tried to sleep with him, saying Tom had come on to him at the bachelor party.

Dev, of course, had played it off. Said it had to be a joke. Said that maybe Tom was drunk. That he hadn't meant it. Maybe Val needed to lighten up too, just like Dev. Of course he was still going through with the wedding. They had people coming. They had paid for everything. They were going to get married and have a wonderful life together. If Val couldn't get on board with that, then maybe he shouldn't come at all.

In the end, Val had attended, sitting in the back row of their outdoor ceremony and leaving before the reception. Dev hadn't seen him again until now.

He hid his cringe at those painful memories, barely, and gritted his teeth as some small part of him pinched with bittersweet yearning for the friendship they'd had and lost, for the innocence that was gone forever, for the ease they used to share together.

All of that was gone.

They were virtual strangers now, and Dev was fine with that.

He wasn't interested in new relationships

of any kind now, thanks to Tom. He'd rebuilt the walls around his heart high and strong and never planned to let them down again. The risk of allowing people close to you, of allowing his emotions to override his common sense, was not worth it.

He was better off alone.

Val continued to stare at him as Dev stepped up to the counter and cleared his throat to catch the attention of a nearby nurse. "Excuse me. I'm Dr. Harrison. I was called down for a pediatric oncology consult. Can you tell me which room it's in, please?"

"I requested the consult," Val said, and Dev's stomach sank to his toes. Of course he had. That just seemed to be the way this day was going. At least Val's brisk voice was all business now as he grabbed a tablet computer from the counter and handed it to Dev before starting off down one of the halls without waiting to see if Dev followed.

After a moment, Dev hurried down the corridor after him, doing his best to study the updated lab results on the tablet instead of remembering all the times he and Val had seen patients together back in residency. Back when everything had been fresh and new, and the possibilities limitless. Nostalgia threatened to overtake him before Dev shoved it firmly aside. The sooner he started treating Val like any other work colleague, the sooner they could put the past behind them and move on.

They reached the last trauma bay on the right, and Val pulled aside a curtain to reveal a teenaged boy on the bed with his mother sitting in a chair beside him. The mother looked understandably worried, given her son's symptoms. Dev had seen the file upstairs in his office before coming down and it could be serious. The monitors hooked up to the patient beeped rhythmically, flashing the teen's vitals in neon green against a backdrop of black as Val made the introductions.

"This is Matthew Warden. He's sixteen and a running back on his high school football team. He presents to the ER today with extreme fatigue, unexplained bruises that aren't sportsrelated, and a persistent fever not responding to OTC meds…"

As he continued, Dev became acutely aware of Val's warmth beside him, penetrating through the material of Dev's lab coat, and with each inhale, he caught a hint of soap from Val's skin.

What the hell?

He didn't want to notice anything about Val other than his medical evaluation of the patient before them. Certainly not how he smelled or felt.

"And this is Dr. Harrison, one of the pediatric oncologists. I've called him in to consult as a precaution, pending the results of the blood work we're running," Val said.

As Dev leaned in to shake hands with both the patient and the mother, his arm inadvertently brushed against Val's and caused an unwanted wave of tingles up the side of Dev's body.

Stop it.

Dev adjusted his glasses and inched away from Val, doing his best not to stare at the dusting of hair on Val's bare forearms. Throat constricted, he asked Matthew, "Have you had any night sweats, Mr. Warden?"

"No. And call me Matt." He crossed his arms over the sheets. "I'm hoping it's just mono."

For Matt's sake, Dev hoped that as well, but he suspected more. "How's your appetite been?"

Ms. Warden answered for her son this time. "He normally eats me out of house and home, but he hasn't been doing that the past two weeks. One of his friends on the team had mono about a month or so ago, so that's why we're hoping it's just that. I know it can be super contagious and Matt said they shared a water bottle after a game."

"That could do it," Val confirmed. "You need to come in contact with their saliva. That's why they call it the kissing disease."

Great. And now Dev had images of kissing Val in his head.

Flustered, Dev stepped over to the bedside to put even more space between him and Val. This was not like him at all, and he needed to get himself under control this instant. He focused on the case and not his racing heart. "Based on the exam results and his history, I'd rather be safe than sorry. I'd say go ahead and isolate him and let's schedule a bone marrow biopsy as well, to cover all our bases."

Val nodded then left to presumably take care of that while Dev pulled on some gloves. "Matt, if you don't mind, I'd like to do a quick exam myself to confirm Dr. Laurent's findings."

"Sure," the kid said, shrugging. "Whatever will get me out of here and back to football practice."

"We'll need to discharge you first for that, and we've still got more tests to run, but I promise we'll do everything we can to get you back to your life outside of here as quickly as possible, Matt." Dev smiled. "Ready?"

Matt nodded.

Dev started by palpating the teen's abdomen, and Matt winced as he pressed lightly over the upper left side of his abdomen just below his rib cage, confirming an enlarged spleen. Next, he checked Matt's ears for signs of infection, but they were clear, as were his throat and lungs. Finally, Dev checked Matt's neck and found several enlarged lymph nodes. Of course, none of those things on their own were proof of anything more serious than mono, but they also didn't rule out acute lymphoblastic leukemia, also called ALL. Only biopsies would do that. He made a mental note to add the lymph nodes to that order.

Finished with the exam, Dev removed his gloves and washed his hands before turning to the patient and his mother, giving them his most comforting smile. "As I said before, we're going to run a few more tests to figure out exactly what we're dealing with here, then we'll know the best treatment for you."

Matt nodded, looking uncertain for the first time since Dev had arrived. "Will that biopsy hurt?"

"It can be a little uncomfortable, yes. But probably nothing worse than you've already experienced on the football field. And we'll do our best to make sure you're as comfortable as possible throughout, okay? We'll take a couple of samples from your neck as well." Dev placed a hand on Matt's shoulder. "We'll take good care of you, I promise."

"Thank you, Dr. Harrison," the mother said, her voice tremulous as she shook Dev's hand again.

"I'm here to help." Dev squeezed her fingers. "I'll review the test results as soon as they become available and keep you both and Dr. Laurent informed of any changes we find. I know the waiting is scary, but I'm committed to getting to the bottom of this."

She smiled, her gaze weary. "I appreciate that, Doctor. My Matthew's been so healthy his whole life. We're not used to spending this much time in hospitals."

"Well, try not to worry," Dev said, giving her as much comfort as he could. Channeling his emotions into his patients and their families was a much safer alternative for him and made him better at his job too. Win-win. "We'll talk again soon."

After leaving Matt and his mother, Dev went to find Val and make sure all his orders were in place, and found him back at the nurses' station. "I confirmed Matthew's spleen is enlarged and tender, as are the lymph nodes in his neck, but his throat, lungs and ears are clear. I'd like to add lymph node biopsies and a lumbar puncture to rule out ALL," Dev told the nurse, then checked his smartwatch before turning back to Val. "I need to get back upstairs to see another patient, but please keep me updated on the results when they come in and we'll go from there."

"I had them schedule an MRI for Matt as well," Val said as Dev headed toward the automatic doors.

"Good." Dev nodded, not turning back for fear of getting lost in Val's blue eyes again. Whatever this ridiculous, odd reaction was, he needed to get it under control before they saw each other again. "Monitor his temperature and blood counts closely. We don't want to miss anything. We'll reconvene after the biopsy results come in."

The doors swished open in front of Dev and before he exited the department, he hazarded one last glance back at Val, only to see him on the phone, bits of his conversation filtering over to Dev, even though he was doing his best not to eavesdrop.

"Hey, Nancy. How's Cam? Still running a fever? Okay." Val ran a hand through his hair, disheveling it, a familiar gesture Dev remembered him doing a lot in residency—a sign he was stressed and trying to hide it. Which made Dev wonder who this Cam person was. Was Val married? Engaged? In a committed relationship with someone? Though he didn't remember seeing a ring on Val's finger.

Not that that meant anything. Doctors frequently removed their rings while treating patients, so...

"Well, make sure Cam stays hydrated, and if his temperature goes up again, call me immediately, okay?" Val continued as the alarm buzzed on the automatic doors and Dev finally stepped out into the hallway, where the elevators were located. The last words that drifted to him before the doors closed again were "Thanks, hon. You're a lifesaver."

Val ended his call and glanced over at Dev through the glass, and Dev looked away fast.

Why am I standing here gawking at the last man on earth I should be interested in?

As he rode back up to his office on the third floor, Dev still felt discombobulated by the whole encounter. He huffed out a breath as the glowing numbers above the door ticked upward, his determination to put it behind him growing as the seconds passed. Whatever strange things seeing Val again had stirred inside him, he needed to deal with because they had a patient to work on together now. And given that they were in the same hospital, Matt wouldn't be the last either. They were both professionals. They could do this, no matter how awkward. He'd come home to focus on his career again and that's exactly what he intended to do. Not get wrapped up in the past. It was all over and done with. The sooner he remembered that, the better.

Val stood at the nurses' station after Dev left, still a bit stunned. When he'd called for the oncology consult, he hadn't paid much attention to who was on call for that department—he just knew he needed one stat for Matthew. So when he'd turned around and saw Dev again after all these years, it had been a real gut punch, to say the least.

Before he got back to work in the ER, Val pulled out his phone again to see a text update from the nanny, Nancy. Cam's temperature was holding steady now and she'd gotten some soup into him, which was good. A bit of the tension in his back eased as he adjusted the stethoscope slung around his neck and made his way back into the fray of the busy department. He still had a few hours left on his shift before he could leave to personally check on his son.

Scanning the list of waiting patients, Val's gaze snagged on Matt's name, then Dev's now listed beside it as consulting oncologist. He'd heard through the grapevine that Dev was back in town, but hadn't expected to see him so soon, and it still seemed unreal. Once upon a time, they'd been about as close as two people could get without sleeping together. He still remembered seeing Dev sitting there at his desk on the first day of medical school, looking so shy and nervous that Val had yearned to make him smile. He'd never imagined that first encounter would lead to years of friendship, nor how it would all end. But even now, he wouldn't have done anything different. He'd been compelled to warn Dev about Tom and the fact he'd come on to him, and he'd do it again, even though it now made working together akin to navigating a minefield of old hurts and resentments.

An image of Dev's face as he'd finally faced Val again after all these years flashed in his head.

He looked good. A bit thinner than he'd been when he'd left ten years ago, but good. Same dark hair and eyes, same lithe build and Tom Ford glasses. There was a new wariness though, a sense of guarded detachedness that Val was sure was meant to keep people away. It only intrigued him more.

Not that he'd indulge that curiosity anytime soon.

Dev had been extremely clear during their last fight that he wanted nothing more to do with Val, and until he heard differently, he had no intention of trying to mend that fence.

Working together on cases would be enough interaction for now.

And, speaking of new cases, he moved between trauma bays over the new few hours, concentrating to keep himself busy and stop worrying about Cam. One of his greatest strengths—or weaknesses, depending on who you asked—was how quickly he connected with people. It had always been something that came easily to him. His sister, Vicki, used to tease him that he could talk to a post, and it was true. He thrived on relationships, felt things deeply. So the last year and half had been especially hard on him since Vicki had died of ovarian cancer and he'd adopted his only nephew, Cam, as his son. Cam's biological father had left shortly before Cam was born, never marrying Vicki or accepting any responsibility for his own child. Val knew from his own childhood growing up in a household with neglectful parents that the world often wasn't fair, but he didn't want that for Cam. The boy was the most important thing in Val's life now and his only family left alive.

For months now, his grief and raising Cam had taken up all his time outside of work, so Val hadn't been connecting socially like he used to, and he missed it. And when he did have time to relax and hang out, the only person he usually did that with was Alex, his late sister's fiancé, who understood what Val and Cam had been through, so it made it easier to not have to explain it all again. There was absolutely nothing romantic between them. Alex was straight. But they were good sounding boards for each other, and had helped each other and Cam through the worst times after the funeral.

Huh. He hadn't really thought about how isolated he'd become, which for an extrovert like him was difficult.

Maybe that's why he was so curious about Dev now, despite knowing that he was off-limits.

And why, when he remembered how close they'd once been, his chest ached for the friend he'd loved like a brother. Sure, if he was honest, he'd always harbored a bit of a crush on Dev, with his whole sexy nerd vibe going on. They'd never crossed that line, but…

Val shook off those inappropriate thoughts and entered a new trauma bay.

Dev could barely look at him today, let alone do anything else.

He needed to keep his feelings to himself.

Waiting for him was an elderly woman named Doris, who'd been brought in by one of the local assisted-living homes. She was complaining of abdominal pain, blood in her stool and weight loss. After running tests to rule out other causes, he got an ultrasound that showed a fecal impaction that both an enema and digital manipulation of the blockage should handle. And that honor fell squarely with one of the new residents. In fact, catching all the fecal-related cases was a rite of passage for the med students around here. Lord knew Val had done his share during that time. He was ready to pass the duty on to the next generation. As he made notes in the patient's chart on his tablet, a nurse poked her head in.

"Dr. Laurent, we need you in trauma bay three," she said.

"On my way." Val turned back to pat Doris's frail hand with a sincere smile. "Don't worry,

Mrs. Carson, we will get you feeling better again soon. Is there anyone we can call for you?"

"My son, please," she said. "He's working downtown. Thank you."

Val got the information and passed it on to someone at the desk before heading to the next case—a twenty-two-year-old man named Bo with a broken arm. After examining the X-rays, he applied a cast with practiced ease, talking the patient through his at-home care as he went. "You'll need to wear this for four weeks, then follow up with Orthopedics. Barring any unforeseen circumstances, you should be good as new."

"Thanks, Doc," Bo said, flashing a relieved grin. "Got to be ready for snowboarding season soon."

"Well, be careful," Val warned as he washed his hands. "Don't want to end up back in here again."

With half an hour left on his shift, Val went to the break room for a bottled water, and the calm between storms allowed thoughts of Dev to creep back in again. He hadn't realized until today how much he'd actually missed the guy until seeing him again. Ten years seemed like a lifetime ago now, and as he bought an energy bar from the vending machine, Val wondered what had brought Dev back home now. Which then led to thoughts of Tom. Ugh. *There* was someone Val would be more than happy never to see again. But if Dev was here, then his husband must be too, right? Though he'd noted Dev hadn't had his wedding ring on today either.

He sat down at a table to eat his quick snack, pondering the situation despite his earlier promise not to. Mentally, he was running on fumes at this point, so he needed to cut himself some slack. Last he'd heard, Tom was running his own successful venture capital company in San Diego, but with the volatile economy these days, maybe something had gone wrong, and the company had folded. Not that he wished anyone ill, but he couldn't imagine it happening to a better guy than Tom. Tom had somehow managed to fool Dev all those years ago, but Val had seen through his phony act from a mile away, especially after the bachelor party.

But if Dev was happy, then that was all that mattered.

The potential what-ifs and what-might-have-beens left Val feeling charged up as he finished his break. He had more than enough on his own plate these days—with Cam sick again and bills to pay and general life stuff as a single dad—than to waste time thinking about things that were none of his business, but still. Whatever this weirdness was between him and Dev, they both needed to get past it if they were going to make this work. For his part, Val was more than ready to move past the awkwardness and back to some semblance of civility.

He stood, yawning and stretching before making his way back to the ER. At thirty-six, pulling these back-to-back twenty-four-hour shifts was getting old. He still had twenty minutes left before he could leave, and he intended to use those to process his day so he didn't take the stress home with him. Cam needed him to be strong, focused and present during their time together, not worrying about the past.

But as soon as he walked back into the department, those plans were shot to hell because a nurse stopped him with an urgent "Dr. Laurent. We need you in trauma bay one."

With a sigh, Val grabbed his tablet from the nurses' station and brought up the patient's file, slipping back into the role he knew best. He followed her down the corridor, donning a fresh gown on the way. "Coming."

CHAPTER TWO

DEV UNLOCKED THE front door of his mother's house that night and walked inside his childhood home. It had been a long, unsettling day, and he wanted nothing more than some peace and quiet to clear his head. Unfortunately, he'd barely made it across the living room when his mother called from down the hall, "Devon, sweetheart. Is that you?"

"Yes. Hi, Mom," he called back, not bothering to mask the weariness edging his voice.

"The delivery service dropped off an envelope for you," she said as she rolled her wheelchair into the room and pointed toward the coffee table. "Looks important. Has a fancy law firm listed as the return address."

"Great." Must be the final divorce papers. Considering how the rest of his day had gone, he probably should have expected they'd show up today. One thing he hadn't really thought through before moving back here was how this place would remind him of his father walking out on them, and how the ones you loved could hurt you, which only made the pain of the divorce sharper. And while his father had never specifically blamed Dev for his leaving, Tom sure had. He'd claimed Dev wasn't giving him what he needed emotionally, and that's why he'd had to seek comfort and solace elsewhere. But it wasn't like he didn't know who Dev was before he'd married him. Hell, before the wedding, he'd actually teased that one day he'd crack Dev's shell. Well, he'd sure done that, Dev supposed. Just not in the way he'd expected. Dev had felt completely shattered after the divorce, but instead of wallowing, he'd quickly reassembled the pieces and sewn them back together stronger and harder than ever. No one was getting into his heart again. No matter how attracted to them he might be, he added, after an image of Val from earlier in the day flickered through his mind. Nope. He was done with romance.

Scowling, he scrubbed a hand over his face, then snatched the envelope off the table and started toward the hallway leading to his old bedroom. "Just what I needed. Thanks."

"Honey, I'm sorry things didn't work out with Tom." His mom watched him as he passed, her expression concerned. "But I hope you don't—"

"Don't what, Mom?" he snapped before he could stop himself. And now he felt worse than before. It wasn't her fault all this was happening. "Don't get angry because he lied and cheated on me? Don't get bitter because it was my own fault for not seeing what he was from the start? Don't close myself off and stop trusting people? Too late for that, Mom. I should have known better. End of story. I won't make the same mistake again. Now, if you'll excuse me."

"Sweetheart—"

"Mom, I really don't want to talk about this tonight, okay?" He stopped at the entrance to the hallway, head down, more exhausted than he could remember in a long time. "Look, I'm sorry I snapped at you. Today has been a lot. I'm going to take a shower then sort through the mess in this envelope. I'll talk to you in the morning."

"I made dinner," his mother called after him. "Yours is in the fridge when you're ready."

"Okay. Thanks," he said. "But I'm not very hungry."

Dev held his breath until the bedroom door closed behind him, then exhaled slowly as blessed isolation wrapped around him like a shroud, a welcome barrier against the world that seemed too loud and too confusing and too cruel for his taste.

Eventually, he shuffled over to the twin bed and sat on the edge, looking around at the space where he'd spent so much time as a kid, building toy models and dreaming of better things. His mom had redecorated in here after he'd married Tom and left for California. The old blue walls were now painted a soothing cream color, and his childhood dark wood furniture had been replaced with light oak and white. Outside the window across from him, autumn leaves rustled in the wind and the old house creaked as if in answer. Then he caught his reflection in the mirror above the dresser, and his sense of failure came roaring back. Dammit. For once, he'd acted recklessly, letting his emotions lead. And look where it had gotten him. Right back where he'd started. The lesson he took from all of this was that love was not worth the risk. He stared at the envelope in his hands and shook his head. More proof of just how blind he'd been about the man he thought he'd loved. Even after Val had tried to tell him. Which only proved he was even more of a fool to trust his own instincts when it came to his feelings. They never led anywhere but trouble for everyone involved. Tom. His dad. Val.

If he'd only kept his feelings out of it, things would've been fine. Or at least no one would've been hurt, especially himself.

With a sigh, he closed his eyes and took a deep breath, pushing his glasses up the bridge of his nose and forcing his tense shoulders to relax. Okay, fine. He honestly couldn't say that if things would've been different, he'd have stuck to cool aloofness, but at least he wouldn't have cared so much when it all fell apart. No. Always keep your armor on was the takeaway here, and he intended to follow that rule going forward. Life was much safer that way.

He blinked down at the envelope in his hand, willing himself to feel nothing. "You were a liar and a cheat, and you cost me everything. Good riddance to you."

The words echoed in the quiet, shadowed room, so different from the home he'd had with Tom in California. Their beach house had always seemed filled with people and light. That was gone now though. He'd let Tom keep the house and all his San Diego friends, in exchange for what he hoped would be peace and quiet, and time to heal back home in Minneapolis. And now that's what he had. Sort of. If he could just get his overanalytical brain to shut off, he'd be all set. He flopped back on the bed to stare up at the ceiling. Things were fine. Or they would be. Just as soon as he got settled and got his head right again. Which meant getting used to having Val around, at least professionally.

A soft knock on the door was followed by his mom poking her head into the room. "Can I come in for a minute?"

Dev shoved the envelope under his pillow, then sat up as she came in with his dinner on a tray across her lap. There were also two mugs of chamomile tea—his favorite—one for him and one for her. The sight of it made a fresh wave of nostalgia squeeze his chest. "Mom, you didn't have to do this. I really am sorry about earlier. I so appreciate you for letting me stay here until I find my own place in town."

"Of course you can stay here, honey. For as long as you need." She smiled as she passed him the tray, minus her own mug. "And it's nice for me to have some help again. Now eat before it gets cold. You're getting too skinny."

He smiled, doing as he was told. Her meat loaf was just as delicious as he remembered growing up. He couldn't remember the last time he'd had a home-cooked meal like this. Tom was out a lot of the time for dinner with clients and Dev didn't really see the point of cooking for one, so he'd ordered in most nights. As he ate, he said, "It's been a long day, and I wasn't expecting to get the divorce papers today. Moving back here has been challenging. Seeing all these reminders of the past."

"You're not having second thoughts, are you?" His mom frowned at him over the rim of her mug. "About Tom, I mean."

"No. God, no." Dev chewed and swallowed another bite of food. With so many things up in the air right now, ending his marriage was the one certainty he had. "I couldn't trust him anymore, Mom. He lied to me repeatedly, from before we were even married. Can't stay with someone after that. Toward the end, the fights… the silence… It was awful." His throat tightened over the last word, and he gulped some tea to ease it. *Awful* was an understatement. *Excruciating* was more like it. All the constant doubts, fears, never knowing who Tom was with or where he was, what to believe. "Like I said, I learned my lesson. I won't make that mistake again."

"Oh, honey." His mother patted his knee. "I'm sorry you had to go through that, but it seems I passed that legacy on to you."

"Legacy?" he asked, frowning as he looked up from his nearly empty plate to her.

"Of dysfunctional relationships." She gave a small shrug. "And you had a hard enough time opening up to people already. I just hope you don't close yourself off completely."

"Why not?" he countered. "I'm perfectly fine on my own. I have a good job, good family. What more do I need? Once I find a place of my own, I'll be set here. Besides, my instincts and emotions are not reliable. That's what got me into this situation in the first place. Better to lead with my head and not my heart, I think, going forward."

A beat passed before his mom responded, watching him. "Sweetheart, I just want to make sure you understand that feeling things is a part of being human. And closing yourself off isn't any safer or healthier than being too open and vulnerable. You have to find the right balance is all. And the right person. Contrary to what that big brain of yours might be telling you, it's not a weakness to trust others, Dev. It's courageous, especially when you have no idea what the outcome will be. Sometimes it works out, sometimes it doesn't. But that doesn't mean you should stop trying." He gave a derisive snort, and she sat back, looking resigned. "Well, whatever happens, I'm just glad you're home, honey. Give yourself some time to heal and relax before you make any big decisions, eh? Because those walls you build around yourself don't just keep out the possibility of pain. They also keep out the possibility of joy. Of love."

Dev put his empty plate and silverware back on the tray, followed by his empty mug after draining his tea in one last, long gulp. Then he stood and headed for the door to take it all back to the kitchen. His mother followed him down the hall. After rinsing his dishes and putting them in the dishwasher, he turned and bent to kiss her cheek. "Thanks again for dinner and the talk, Mom. Now, I need to take a shower and get in bed before I fall over. Good night."

"'Night," she called after him, and he headed back to his room.

The long, steamy shower helped ease away some stress. Afterward, he wrapped a towel around his waist and stood at the sink to brush his teeth, staring at himself in the mirror. Dark eyes lined with stress, stubble-covered jaw, shadows under his cheekbones. His mom was right. He was too skinny.

It's not a weakness to trust others, Dev. It's courageous, especially when you have no idea what the outcome will be.

Maybe she was right, but it didn't feel like that right now. In fact, Dev wasn't sure he'd ever let go of that tight control over his emotions again. He wasn't sure he even knew how.

Across town, nestled in a cozy bedroom painted blue, Val sat propped up against a mountain of pillows with a well-worn copy of *The Velveteen Rabbit* in his hand and his son curled beside him beneath a heap of blankets. The boy's eyes were wide and attentive, despite the pallor of his cheeks. His cold seemed unchanged from the last time Val had checked him.

"Does it hurt?" Cam asked, his voice small but earnest. "Being real, I mean?"

Val paused, considering the story's deeper meaning. Since Vicki's passing, it had become Cam's favorite, so he wanted to choose his answer wisely. "Sometimes. But being real is also worth it. Because when you're real, authentic, you can truly love and be loved in return. And that's worth any risk."

Cam seemed to take a moment to process that new information. "What about when someone dies? Do they stop being real?"

Val's heart clenched. Hard as it had been for him to lose his older sister, poor Cam had lost his mother and no amount of love and connection from Val could ever fill that void, though he tried his best. One of the reasons he'd gone ahead and adopted Cam was to give him a sense of stability and to reassure the boy that Val had no intention of leaving him anytime soon. "No, buddy. Those who pass on will always be real, and the love we have for them stays with us forever. That's the magic part—you carry them with you for eternity."

"Mommy is here with me now then?"

"Always, buddy." Cam's hopeful tone pinched Val's heart and he pulled the boy in for a hug. "She's always with you."

"Okay." Cam snuggled beneath the covers then, his eyelids slowly lowering as sleep beckoned. "Love is forever."

"Forever and ever." Val set the book aside and extricated himself carefully, smiling as he kissed his son's forehead, then shut off the light, the soft glow of the night-light casting soft shadows across the room. "Now, get some sleep. You need your rest to heal."

He was almost out the door when Cam asked quietly from behind him, "Do you miss her a lot?"

"Every day, buddy," Val said, his voice rough. Vicki had been the center of both of their lives since Dev had left. She'd been so vibrant and full of life right up until the disease took her too soon.

"Does it get easier? The missing?" Cam peeked out from under the blanket to meet Val's gaze.

Chest tight, he swallowed hard, trying to figure out the best way to talk about grief with a child. "It changes," he said finally. "Like…carrying a pebble in your pocket. At first, it feels heavy, and you're aware of it constantly. But over time, it just becomes a normal part of you. Then you don't notice the weight as much, but you never forget it's there."

Cam nodded, looking solemn. "I know you said she's here, but I wish I could see her again, even for a little while."

"Me too, buddy," Val said from the doorway. "But we still have each other, right?"

"Yeah," Cam said. "You won't leave me, will you?"

The question, laden with the fear of further loss, was another stab in Val's heart.

"I don't plan on going anywhere, Cam. Promise," Val vowed "We have each other. Nothing will change that, no matter what happens."

"Good," Cam murmured, closing his eyes at last. "'Night, Uncle Val."

"'Night." Val hesitated before closing the door, watching over the boy who'd become his world. As the night settled, his thoughts snagged on how quickly time passed when you weren't paying attention, how precious the moments were, how quickly they could slip away.

He walked through the quiet house, checking the front and back doors to make sure they were locked. As he flopped down on the couch in the living room to watch TV, he realized how lonely his life had become. For a guy who'd always been surrounded by friends, it was a bit disconcerting. It wasn't like he didn't go out sometimes after work, have a casual drink or a dance. And, of course, Alex still came over once in a while when he wasn't traveling for his job to spend time with Cam and check in on Val. But honestly, other than Vicki, no one had ever been as close to him as Dev…

God, Dev.

He wondered what Dev was doing right now. Was he sitting alone too, thinking about Val? He snorted and shook his head. Given how cold Dev had been toward him earlier, that was probably a no. Which meant he needed to face facts. It might be too late to change things between him and Dev, and the sooner Val accepted that, the sooner they could all move on.

Now, if he could just get the message through to his heart to stop caring, he'd be all set.

CHAPTER THREE

"WE'VE GOT ONE MORE PATIENT, Dr. Harrison," the nurse said as Dev washed his hands.

"Great. Tell them I'll be right in," Dev said over his shoulder. When he'd taken the position at the MCC, part of his responsibilities was to volunteer in the staff clinic once a month, and tonight was his night. It was a nice service the hospital offered their employees and their families, and most of the cases he saw were kids needing shots or school physicals, with the occasional cold and ear infection thrown in for fun. It was nice to keep his skills sharp and see patients with less ominous diagnoses than were usually on his roster.

He dried his hands then picked up the tablet the nurse had left for him with the patient's file without glancing at it, and headed into the next room. It was in a corridor that had formerly held a private practice that had since been vacated and was now used for the monthly clinic.

A check of his smartwatch said it was almost closing time, so once he finished with this case, he could go home and rest.

"Hello, I'm Dr. Dev Harrison," he said as he opened the door. "How can I—"

Dev stopped in his tracks at the sight of Val sitting there beside a small boy with the same tawny hair and blue eyes on the table. Stunned speechless, he just blinked at them both until Val finally broke the silence.

"Uh...hi," Val said, standing and rubbing his palms on the legs of his jeans. He must not have worked today, Dev thought absently. "Cam here is on his third cold in a month and a half and while the OTC meds have helped, I'd just like to have him checked out by a fresh set of eyes to make sure he's good to go back to school tomorrow."

"Are you a doctor like Uncle Val?" the boy asked, finally snapping Dev out of his stupor. Uncle Val? Right. This must be Vicki's son. He'd been born after Dev had moved to California, but his mom had mentioned him in her emails. The boy must be living with Val now after Vicki's passing.

Dev cleared his throat and finally looked at the file. Cameron Laurent. Seven years old. According to the file, the boy had had several colds over the past few months but was feeling better now. Vitals were normal and he had no complaints today. Good. That was good. Because it meant Dev could hopefully get this exam finished quickly and get out of here because he could feel Val watching him like a physical weight on his shoulders. Gah. Despite his wishes, he was still far too aware of the man than he wanted to be.

Get a grip. Get this over with. Get out.

Dev turned away to set the tablet aside and pull on his gloves, affixing his most professional demeanor to hide the swirl of disorder inside him. When he turned back, he was all business, ignoring Val completely to focus on his patient. "Yes, I'm a doctor. But I'm a pediatric oncologist."

The boy scrunched his nose, continuing to play with the toy he'd brought with him, a Lego figurine of a Transformers character, if Dev wasn't mistaken. He kept abreast of the latest toys as much as possible for relating to his young patients. Plus, Lego sets were just cool. "What's that?"

"I normally treat children with cancer," he said, stepping closer. "But today I'm volunteering down here in the clinic. Cameron, do you mind if I examine you?"

"No," the boy said, glancing up at Dev. "And people call me Cam. My mom had cancer."

"Okay, Cam," Dev said, cringing inwardly at his blunder. Normally, he had way more tact, but he felt knocked off-kilter by Val showing up again so unexpectedly. "And I'm very sorry about your mother. I knew her and she was a great lady."

"Everyone says that." Cam frowned down at his toy. "I miss her a lot sometimes."

"I bet you do."

Cam nodded. "She always made me laugh."

"Me too," Dev agreed. Vicki had always been so full of energy and light.

"So, how'd you know my mom?" Cam looked so much like Val that if Dev didn't know better, he'd think the boy was his biological son. Same tawny hair, same blue eyes, same disarming smile. "Was she your friend?"

"She was," Dev said, his voice turning gruff again before he swallowed hard. "I spent a lot of time at her house during medical school."

"Then you were friends with Uncle Val too?" Cam asked, looking back up at Dev again before he turned to his uncle with an excited grin. "Are you guys friends too?"

"Oh…uh…" Val said.

At the same time, Dev said, "We used to be."

"Let's get this exam done then, shall we?" Flustered, Dev pulled an otoscope from his pocket and focused on his patient instead of Val, who stood to the side, close enough that Dev was aware of his every movement. Or at least it seemed that way. His pulse tripped before he forced himself to calm down. "Ears look clear," he said to no one in particular. He grabbed a tongue depressor from a canister on the counter. "Say *ah*, please."

Cam did so and Dev checked the boy's throat next. "Throat clear as well."

"Like I said," Val said into the uncomfortable tension between them as Dev palpated the lymph nodes in Cam's neck. "He's had a couple of colds, and I just wanted him cleared before I send him back to school tomorrow. Nancy's been watching him all day and said he's been fine, but I wanted fresh eyes. My shift ended a few hours ago, so I ran home and changed and brought him back here to the clinic, thinking it would be faster than trying to get a last-minute appointment with his regular pediatrician, so…" Val's voice trailed off as if he realized he'd been babbling. "Anyway, thanks for seeing him."

Dev took the stethoscope from around his neck to listen to the boy's breathing. Clear as well. Cam seemed good to go. Dev documented it all in the file, then told Val as much.

"Do you like Lego, Dr. Harrison?" Cam asked as Dev took off his gloves and washed his hands again.

"I do," Dev said, grabbing several paper towels from the dispenser, glad for something to concentrate on beside Val. "I used to love them as a kid too, but they weren't as fancy as the one you have there. Is that a Transformer?"

"It is!" Cam unfolded a set of wings from the back of the toy. "These have to be strong enough to fly through space."

"Very true," Dev said, knowing that play was an important part of healing for many grieving young patients. "Strong wings for a strong journey. Do you have a favorite Lego set?"

"I like anything space!" Cam said. "I'm just starting the new Mandalorian N-1 Starfighter Microfighter set now. Uncle Val says I go through them too fast. He says I'm going to bankrupt him one day." Those sets could be very expensive, sometimes upward of several hundred dollars for the collector sets, so Dev couldn't help chuckling at that. His laughter ended abruptly at Cam's next words. "You should come over to our house and help me build it. Can he come over, Uncle Val?"

Both men looked at each other, then away fast.

"Okay, buddy. I'm sure Dr. Harrison is way too busy to build toys with you right now," Val said, picking up the boy and setting him on his feet on the floor. "I think you've got a clean bill of health to return to school in the morning. Why don't you go out and play in the waiting room, Cam, while I finish up with Dr. Harrison."

"Okay," the boy said agreeably. "And don't forget to ask about coming over! Bye, Dr. Dev. Is it okay if I call you that, Dr. Harrison?"

"Uh, sure," Dev said, resisting the urge to run a finger under his collar. When had it gotten so hot in here? "That's fine, Cam."

"Okay. Bye, Dr. Dev!" Cam took off then, leaving another awkward silence in his wake.

Alone with Val again, Dev turned back toward the counter to type his notes into the chart on his tablet while Val shuffled from foot to foot beside him, looking about as uncomfortable as Dev felt.

"Look, I didn't plan this at all, I swear. I had no idea you'd be manning the clinic tonight," Val said. "Like I said, I just thought it would be easier bringing him here."

"It's fine." Dev finished his notes then scribbled a quick note of clearance for Cam to take back to school with him the next day, praying for a swift escape. "Have a good night, Dr. Laurent. Oh, and I'd suggest getting a humidifier for Cam's room with the drier winter air coming."

He turned on his heels then and walked away, only to find Val following him. The man had always been persistent. Dev finally stopped at the empty nurses' station and turned back to Val. He needed this to be over so he could collect himself again. Spending too much time around Val was dangerous to his plans to stay distant. "Was there something else you needed?"

Val huffed out a breath then scrubbed his hands over his face. "Look, Dev. About Tom. I know you didn't want to hear it, but now that we're working together again, I really think we should clear the air once and for all. I'm sorry about how things ended between us all those years ago. When I told you about Tom coming on to me, I wasn't trying to hurt you. I was just trying to look out for you. I hope that you and Tom can forgive me, and we can all move on from here."

Oh, God.

Dev realized that Val didn't know about the divorce. And how would he? They'd barely spoken to each other since Dev's return to Minneapolis and, even then, only about the cases they were working on together. Right. Jaw tight, Dev forced out the words. "Not that it's any of your business, but Tom and I are divorced. I just sent the signed papers back. He cheated on me during our marriage. Repeatedly. Congratulations. You were right about him all along."

All the shame and embarrassment curdled inside him like sludge as he steeled himself for Val's I-told-you-so reaction. Dev should have known. Should have listened. Would have saved himself a lot of pain, but he'd been in love. Or what he'd thought was love. *Never again.* But when he finally hazarded a glance at Val, all he saw was sympathy.

"Oh, no. I'm so sorry, Dev."

"Yes, well. It's over and done now. Water under the bridge. I've moved on." Dev turned back around and sucked in a breath, wishing to God that was true. But maybe if he willed it enough, it would become so… "And apology accepted. I should have heeded your warnings back then. Would've saved me a lot of wasted time."

Val just stood there, looking like he wanted to say more, but wasn't sure if he should. Finally, he sighed. "For what it's worth, I'm glad you're home, Dev. And I hope we can start fresh now.

Thank you again for checking on Cam. I know he's in good hands with you."

Dev only nodded then, not trusting his voice as he pushed his glasses up the bridge of his nose again, memories of the past lingering like a fine mist between them. "Thank you."

Neither of them moved, eyes locked, until a small voice called down the hall.

"Uncle Val, can we stop for ice cream on the way home? I ate all my peas at dinner. Ask Nancy."

Val finally tore his gaze from Dev's and called back over his shoulder. "All right, buddy. You've been a good patient tonight, so…" Then he turned back to Dev with a twinkle in his eye. Dev hadn't realized how much he'd missed seeing that mischievousness until now. He tamped that down fast. He had no business missing Val or his twinkle. "If you're done here, do you want to go for ice cream with us? I know a place that has the best Moose Tracks in town. My treat. Consider it a peace offering."

"Oh, I…" Not expecting the invitation and not sure what to say, Dev checked his smartwatch, more to give himself a moment to think of a way to get out of it than anything else. It was going on 8:00 p.m. He could claim his mother needed him for something, or that he had an early call in the morning. But when he opened his mouth, what came out was "Okay."

What the hell is wrong with me?

Val gave him a bright grin then and the whole room seemed to lighten around Dev. Which was just plain ridiculous. He scowled, annoyed with himself for getting himself in this situation. "I'll need to finish up here first."

"Don't worry, Doc," said the nurse who'd been giving shots all day as she walked out of the room Dev had seen Cam in. "I've got everything cleaned up and ready to go for next week. You go ahead. I'll lock up here."

Perfect.

Teeth gritted, Dev gave a curt nod. "Guess I'm ready to go then."

He pulled on his coat then followed Val out to the waiting room, where Cam cheered with excitement when he found out Dev was going with them for ice cream. They walked outside into the chilly night air, Dev grateful for the coolness on his heated skin. "Where is this place?"

"Not far. Do you want to ride together?" Val asked as they stopped near a shiny new SUV.

"No," Dev said. It was one thing to suffer through a quick snack with Val. Riding in a confined space with him would be entirely too much for Dev at this point. His stupid insides were already quivering in anticipation for some reason that Dev didn't want to think too much about. "I'll drive too. I can't stay long."

"Okay," Val said agreeably. "Where are you parked?"

Dev pointed to the gray sedan he was renting until he got settled and bought something permanent. "I'll follow you."

A few minutes later, they pulled up outside a nondescript white building on Upton Avenue and parked at the curb. Cam was the first out, hopping on the sidewalk, while Val and Dev locked up their vehicles then followed him inside the local shop. From all the signs, Dev gathered they made homemade ice cream in unique flavors, along with specialty coffees and baked goods. The air smelled of sugar and waffle cones, and a scattering of round tables filled a brightly lit area with people laughing and chatting over their desserts. Dev didn't remember the place from before his move, but he'd been gone a while, so...

"What flavor are you getting tonight, buddy?" Val asked Cam, holding him by the shoulders in front of him as they stood looking up at the handwritten menu boards hanging behind the counter.

"Oreo!" Cam clapped excitedly. "In a chocolate cone, please."

"Did you get that?" Val asked the guy at the register, who nodded and grinned at Cam. "And for you?" the cashier asked Val.

"Moose Tracks in a plain waffle cone, please," Val said, then looked back at Dev. "What about you?"

Dev read all the selections, and they all sounded good, but he decided to indulge his chocolate cravings tonight. He chose the one listed as being filled with fudge, truffles, chunks of Heath Bar and a dash of sea salt. He deserved it after all the stress he was putting himself through here. "A scoop of the Nicollet Avenue Pothole, please. In a waffle bowl."

"You got it, sir," the cashier said, then rang up the order for Val and directed them to the other end of the counter to wait on their orders. They stood in line and soon carried a tray with their goodies to a table in the far corner.

Once they were all seated and had their ice cream, Dev sat back and ate, listening in as Val and Cam chatted about their days, zoning out a bit as he went into a chocolate coma from the most delicious ice cream he'd ever had in his life. So much so that when he did manage to tune back in to the conversation, he found both Val and Cam looking at him expectantly.

Whoops. They'd obviously asked him something.

"Sorry, I didn't catch that," Dev said, sitting forward to finish his dessert.

"I asked where you were living," Val said. "Cam and I are in Vicki's old place."

"Oh. I'm staying at my mother's right now until I find someplace."

"How is your mom?" Val asked. "I haven't seen her since the funeral."

"Good," Dev said, glad for a neutral topic to discuss. "Her MS is under control right now, though she's in a wheelchair, as I'm sure you saw. She's still upbeat and positive though. She's glad to have me back in town to help out when she needs."

"I'm sure she is." Val smiled. "You know, I still keep in touch with some of the old gang from medical school who are in town. We try to get together at least once a month for dinner and drinks. If you're interested, I can let you know the next time we go out. I'm sure everyone would love to see you."

The last thing Dev wanted to do was spend an evening answering a bunch of uncomfortable questions about things he was trying to forget, so he kept his response as noncommittal as possible. "I'll have to check my schedule. Things are a bit chaotic right now, schedule-wise."

"Understood." Val reached for a napkin from the dispenser in the center of the table at the same time Dev did, and their fingers brushed, the slight contact another unwanted jolt of awareness up Dev's arm. He pulled back fast, frowning. The ink was barely dry on his divorce papers. He didn't want to get involved with anyone again, let alone Val. He needed to stop this nonsense before it got out of hand.

He mumbled an apology and waited for Val to get his napkin before reaching for one himself. He wasn't sure exactly why Val was affecting him this way now, but he didn't like it. Not at all. It made no sense. They'd been friends for years before the falling-out and not once had he been attracted to Val like this. What was wrong now that this was happening? Had something short-circuited in his brain after the divorce? Had Tom permanently broken him? Or, worst of all, was he actually interested in Val that way? No. No, he couldn't be. He'd vowed never to get involved with anyone like that again. Never to let anyone close like that again. Must be his wonky instincts again, leading him down the path to rack and ruin.

Thankfully, both Val and Cam seemed oblivious to Dev's inner turmoil as they continued chatting about some project Cam was working on at school. Dev was glad for the reprieve, watching them interact from beneath his lashes. Val seemed like a good parent, attentive and sweet, ruffling the boy's hair when Cam said something funny, valuing his ideas and opinions. Dev would've given anything for a dad like that at Cam's age…

"Dev?" Val asked, pulling him back to the present again as Cam slid off his stool to take their empty tray back to the counter. "Everything okay?"

"What?" Devon frowned down at the table. He'd devoured his edible bowl while he'd been lost in his thoughts and didn't even remember eating it. "Sorry."

"Don't apologize," Val said, standing when Cam returned to the table. "I just asked if you needed anything. I know it can be a lot, starting over again. And with the crazy schedule you mentioned, if you need help with anything, just let me know."

They all pulled their coats back on and headed for the exit. This hadn't been as horrible as Dev had expected. Not that he planned to repeat it or anything. "I really do need to get home now. Thanks for the ice cream."

"My pleasure." Val held the door for them, then stood on the sidewalk outside with Dev as Cam climbed into the SUV. "I'm glad we cleared things up."

"Me too." Dev turned toward his car. "Good night. Bye, Cam."

"Bye, Dr. Dev," the boy called before closing the door on the SUV.

"'Night," Val called from behind Dev, then added, "Hey, if you're not busy next weekend, I've got season tickets to the Timberwolves. It's their home opener. I have an extra ticket this time, so if you want to come with me and Cam, I'm sure he'd love it, and you'd save the ticket from going to waste…"

It sounded like an innocent enough invitation. Practical too, since season tickets to an NBA game were not cheap, but Dev had to stick to his plans. Still, he didn't want to be rude after he and Val had just reached an accord, so he went with his usual nonanswer. "I'll have to check my schedule."

"Great," Val said, waving as Dev reached his car at the curb. "I'll text you the details just in case."

City lights blurred past as Dev drove home,

the hum of the car's engine soothing away a bit of the tension that had lingered within him ever since he'd left San Diego. Even though this evening hadn't gone the way he'd expected at all, it had been oddly relaxing. In the months since he and Tom had separated, he'd been so guarded, losing himself in work to avoid dealing with the loss of the future he'd thought they'd have had together. But tonight, something had shifted a little inside him, making him think that perhaps he would be okay on his own after all.

He stopped at a red light and glanced up at the night sky through the window. The stars were pinpricks of light against the vast darkness, and for the first time in a long time, Dev allowed himself to just take it in, to let go of his tight control. Not all the way, never all the way, not anymore, but a tiny crack appeared in his walls just the same.

Dev was still contemplating it all when he arrived back home at his mom's. He walked in to find her watching a special celebrity prime-time episode of *Jeopardy!*, calling out answers to the people on screen as she worked on her knitting. He took off his coat and sat on the couch, not quite ready to go to bed.

When a commercial break came on, his

mom glanced over at him. "How was your day, honey?"

"Interesting," he said, distracted.

"Interesting good or interesting bad?" she asked over the steady *clack-clack* of her knitting needles.

"I'm not sure yet. I volunteered at the staff clinic tonight and Val showed up with his son, Cam. Did you know he'd adopted Vicki's boy?"

"Of course." His mom smiled. "He couldn't have a better father."

Dev frowned. "And you didn't think to mention it to me?"

"I guess it never came up," she said, shrugging slightly. "Why? Is it important to you?"

"No." He scowled. "Yes. I don't know. It would have been nice not to be blindsided is all."

His mother raised a skeptical brow at him. "Sure. Okay. And how was it seeing him again?"

Wasn't that the question of the night? Dev exhaled slowly. "Fine. We'd actually worked on a case together in the ER, so it wasn't like we haven't talked at all since I've been back. And Cam is a very sweet boy. He reminds me a lot of Vicki." Dev found himself smiling. "He loves Lego."

"Sounds like someone else I know when he

was that age," his mom said, echoing Dev's own thoughts. "I know you can't tell me specifics, but I hope Cam is okay?"

"He's fine," Dev said, staring at the TV screen where the new host was talking to the contestants about the charities they were supporting with their winnings. "We went for ice cream afterward."

"Really?" His mom stopped knitting and leaned forward, her sudden interest making his cheeks heat. "And how did that go?"

"Fine," Dev snapped, more annoyed with himself than anything. For some frustrating reason, he couldn't seem to stop himself from becoming a blushing schoolboy now whenever he discussed Val. It was embarrassing. "I'm a grown man," he said, as much for his mother's benefit as his own. "I can certainly handle myself through a brief encounter at an ice-cream parlor."

"Glad to hear it," his mother said, chuckling as she sat back and resumed her knitting. "Where'd you go?"

He gave her the name. "I don't remember it from when I lived here before. So much has changed in the city since I've been gone."

"You can say that again." She grinned. "I'm glad you're starting to get out again and explore it all. Sounds like having Val back in your life is good for you."

"I don't know about that," Dev argued, agitated by the spike of adrenaline in his bloodstream. Yes, he'd enjoyed their trip to get ice cream. Didn't mean he planned to repeat it.

Do I?

No. That would just be asking for trouble, and Dev had had enough of that for a lifetime.

Still, he couldn't seem to stop himself from mentioning, "He invited me to go with him and Cam to a Timberwolves game this weekend."

"Excellent." His mother grinned wider. "I went to one last season with my church group, and it was great fun."

"I'm not going," Dev said, steadfast in his decision. He had no business continuing to socialize with Val and Cam when it would never come to anything. "I'll probably be on call anyway."

He wasn't on call. The schedule for his practice had already been posted earlier that day, and Dev had Saturday off. But it sounded like as good an excuse as any.

"Well, if you're not going, I'd seriously consider it. Those tickets are hard to come by and I think you'd really enjoy yourself. Get you out and about again. Do you good. And you don't know many people in town yet. Val is nothing if not social. He could help you meet new people."

Dev couldn't argue with that. Val had always been the extrovert friend he'd relied on back in medical school to drag him out of the house and to whatever events were happening. He'd almost always enjoyed himself when he got there, and he would have missed it all if Val hadn't brought him along.

He took a deep breath. As part of his hiring into the hospital, he'd promised not only to volunteer at the staff clinic but also to volunteer at other community events and charities to help promote the practice's health-care initiatives, so maybe his mother was right. Maybe Val could be his first step into that world. And yes, it would mean controlling his errant reactions for another evening, but then Dev had had a lot of practice doing that, didn't he?

Still, he wasn't quite ready to commit yet. He needed to consider it more beforehand. He pushed to his feet and headed for the hallway. "I'll think about it."

"Hey," Val said, stepping aside and holding the front door open for Alex, who walked in holding a large pizza box with a two-liter bottle of soda balanced precariously atop it. As he passed, the air filled with the delicious scents of baked cheese and veggies, and Val's stomach growled loudly. "Smells great."

"I know, right?" Alex said, hiking his chin toward the bottle. "Can you grab that?"

Val shut the door then did as he'd been asked, carrying it to the kitchen table where plates and napkins had already been set out in preparation for their meal. As he got out glasses and filled them with ice, Alex set the pizza box in the center of the table. Val called down the hall, "Dinner's here, Cam."

The next few seconds were filled with an excited seven-year-old racing down the hall and into Alex's arms, and Alex swinging him around like he weighed nothing. The guy was a salesman but built like a lumberjack, big and burly with the beard to match.

"Hey, kiddo," Alex said, setting Cam down at last. "How goes it?"

Cam proceeded to fill Alex in on basically everything that had happened to him that week while they all took a seat and filled their plates with pizza and Val filled their glasses with soda. He'd just come off another twenty-four-hour shift and he appreciated not having to worry about dinner more than he could say. When Alex had called earlier and asked if tonight was good for him to stop by for their monthly meetup, Val had jumped at the chance.

"So," Alex said once Val had taken his seat and was pulling his first slice out of the box. "What was it like seeing your old friend again?"

Val had been trying to answer that himself in the days since the clinic and the ice cream afterward. He still hadn't landed on a clear answer yet, so he went with a shrug and a "It was nice."

"Nice?" Alex gave him a flat look. "That's it?"

"What do you want me to say?" Val asked after swallowing a large bite of deluxe pizza. "It was fine. We haven't seen each other in ten years and we've both changed a lot, so it was a little awkward at first, but we're both adults and we dealt with it. And we'd already worked on a case together at work, so it wasn't like it was the first time we had seen each other again, so it wasn't a big deal. End of story."

If only that were true…

"How'd you meet, Uncle Val?" Cam asked, a big dollop of sauce dripping off the pizza in his hand and on to the front of his shirt. "Oops!"

Val reached over with a napkin to clean him up. He'd have to mention that stain to Nancy when she did laundry next time to make sure she soaked it. Hopefully tomato came out. That shirt was brand-new. "We met in med school," Val said, as he dabbed at the stain with his own napkin wet with his spit. "On our first day. I walked in and saw Dev alone in the corner and felt sorry for him, so I made it my mission to be his friend. Just like I told you to do at school. Not everyone is as comfortable socially around other people as we are, so we need to meet them where they are and help them be comfortable."

"That's how I met Benjamin," Cam said, nodding. "He's a good friend."

"He is." Val sat back, giving up on the stain for now. He smiled at Cam then turned back to Alex. "Seriously. It was just a nice gesture to help ease the awkwardness between us after what happened."

"What happened?" Cam asked innocently.

"Nothing you need to worry about, kiddo," Alex intervened, ruffling Cam's hair. "Tell me about your new Lego set."

That, thankfully, set Cam off on a whole other tangent, going on and on about Microfighters and *Star Wars* and the next show that was coming out soon on streaming. Val had a hard time keeping up with it all and didn't try. He loved sci-fi as much as the next person, but Cam took it to a whole new level, so he just indulged his son and loved that he loved it all so much. He wouldn't be surprised if Cam walked on Mars someday, he was that focused on science and space. And he was happy to encourage that in whatever way he could.

By the time they finished the meal and Val cleaned up then got Cam ready for bed, Alex was sitting in the living room, having picked up and put away all the scattered toys from earlier. He really was a good friend. Val sank down tiredly on the other end of the sofa from him and rested his head against the cushions.

"So, now tell me how it really was, seeing this guy again," Alex said. "And don't give me that 'nice' BS. That won't cut it."

"Honestly? I'm still trying to figure it out myself," Val said truthfully. He and Alex talked regularly about everything they were going through. It was a bond forged when they'd gone through it all with Vicki together, and one they still treasured now as they ventured back out into the world post-loss. Alex was dipping his toe back into dating again after more than a year, and Val helped advise him with that as best he could, since he hadn't really dated anyone since Vicki's passing himself. He was too busy with work and Cam and adjusting to life as a single dad. But sometimes just having fresh eyes on things helped, and Val was happy to be that for Alex—and hoped for the same in return now. "I told you about the fight we had after Dev's then-fiancé came on to me at the bachelor party. Back then he didn't believe me. But I'm pretty sure he does now, since they're divorced. He said Tom cheated on him. Repeatedly."

"Oh, wow." Alex's eyes widened. "And what did you say?"

"That I was sorry. Which I am. I'm sorry Dev had to go through all that. Tom never deserved Dev, and I hope the guy is attacked by a swarm of killer bees for hurting Dev."

Alex snorted. "Tell me how you really feel."

"The bee-nado didn't cover it?" Val laughed. "Enough about that a-hole though. He doesn't deserve the attention. It's Dev who's important now."

"How important?" Alex pushed. He'd never let Val off easy before, so he knew better than to expect it now. "You said it was awkward seeing him again. Do you want to reconnect?"

"I do," Val said without reservation. "After what he's been through, I'm sure he could use a friend."

"And that's all it is? Friendship?"

"Of course." Val frowned. "What else would it be?"

"I don't know. That's why I'm asking," Alex

countered, looking innocent enough, though Val suspected more beneath that question.

Or maybe that was just him reading more into it than he should, a frequent problem he had. Reading more into things, feeling things more deeply than he should, caring too much. He liked to genuinely connect with people, that was all. It was the same with Dev. He'd missed that connection, and he wanted it back. That was all. And if some tiny part of him might wish for more, well, that was too bad. Dev was clearly avoiding anything like that, and Val would honor those boundaries. Period.

"Just friendship," he said, as much for Alex as himself. "I invited him to the Timberwolves game Saturday, since you bailed on me."

"Hey, I can't help it if work requires me at a conference in Las Vegas the next day." Alex shrugged. "Did he take you up on your offer?"

"Not yet." It had been three days since the ice cream encounter on Monday night, and each time Val checked his messages on his phone, there'd been nothing—despite him sending Dev the details on Tuesday. It was okay, he told himself. Dev would let him know when he was ready. If he was ready. He wasn't holding out hope though. "If he doesn't want to go, it's fine. I wanted to offer though. He hasn't been back long and probably doesn't know many people here now, so I wanted to make him feel welcome."

"Uh-huh." Alex snorted. "Whatever."

"What?" Val sat up and smacked his friend with one of the throw pillows between them. "I'm a friendly guy."

His phone buzzed in his pocket then and he pulled it out, expecting an update on one of his patients from the ER. What he saw onscreen though froze him to the spot.

Alex paused midretaliation with a throw pillow in his hand, noticing how still Val had gotten. "What? Something wrong?"

"Uh…no. I don't think so," he said, unable to keep the astonishment from his voice. "Dev just texted me back. He's going to the game on Saturday with us."

"Wow." Alex barked out a laugh and set his throw pillow aside. "Well, that's good news then, right?"

"Sure," Val said, still a bit dazed. He'd basically given up on the invitation, but now, his heart was racing a million miles a minute even though he knew it shouldn't be. It was just a game, just an evening between friends, as he'd told Alex. So why did it feel like more? "It's good."

* * *

Saturday late afternoon found Val standing in a large crowd, entering the Target Center arena beside Dev, still stunned the guy had actually shown up. Sure, he'd texted Val and told him he would, but they hadn't had a chance to talk in person since, and Val had half expected that Dev would cancel at the last minute. But he hadn't, and sure enough, when he and Cam had arrived at their appointed meetup spot, Dev had been waiting there, early as always, looking as uncomfortable as a fart in church, as Vicki would have said. Cam had been thrilled to see Dr. Dev again, of course, and had rushed to hug Dev's legs. The kid had inherited Val's gift of the gab and collecting people, it seemed, and he made friends wherever he went. Plus, after Dev had confessed to a love of Lego too, he'd become Cam's new favorite obsession, apparently. The kid hadn't stopped talking about this game since Val had told him the news that Dev would be joining them this morning.

And speaking of obsessions…

Val glanced over at Dev for the umpteenth time as they now made their way inside with the rest of the throng of Timberwolves fans, like he still needed proof this was really happening. And yep. It was. The clamor of excitement reverberating through the stadium matched the zing of electricity inside Val's own bloodstream. Chances were slim that even though Dev had finally accepted his apology the other night, they'd just fall back easily into the friendship they'd had before. But if they could at least keep things lighter between them now, Val would be grateful.

He'd had enough darkness since the funeral to last him a lifetime.

Cam, who stood between him and Dev and clasped each of their hands to avoid getting lost, stared around them with wonder at the sea of blue jersey-wearing fans milling around. He'd been too young to bring here when Vicki was still alive, and then after she'd passed, the timing hadn't been right. Tonight was Cam's first time at a real NBA game, though he watched them on TV with Val when they could. He'd even bought them each a new official jersey to wear today. He would have gotten one for Dev too, but he wasn't sure of the size or if he'd even want one so... Dev wore his usual jeans and sweater, an island of calm amidst the frenetic energy of game night, and damn if he still didn't have his whole sexy nerd thing going on, even after all these years, which had always hit Val's sweet spot, even though they'd never crossed that line.

And wouldn't now, he reminded himself.

This was about friendship, like he'd told Alex. Showing Dev around. Nothing more.

Besides, even sixteen months later, Val still felt like he was processing his grief over losing his sister and adjusting to his new life with Cam. Most of the time, he barely had time to breathe, let alone the time for a fling or anything more. And sure, sometimes he missed having that close connection with someone, a special person who knew him better than anyone else and loved him anyway, but he wouldn't trade his life with Cam now for anything in the world. He had Alex, sure, but some small part of him still yearned for more... And if he was lonely, well, he'd get over it.

"Look, Uncle Val! There's Crunch the Wolf!" Cam's voice cut through his thoughts as his son pointed to the team's mascot bouncing between laughing, cheering fans.

"You want to say hi to him?" Val asked, crouching beside the boy. Dev watched them, his dark gaze lingering on their interaction, a ghost of a smile tugging at the corner of his lips as something flashed across his features, so quick Val couldn't quite read it, but it made his chest pinch anyway.

"Yes, please!" Cam jumped up and down, obviously feeling better than he had the other day.

By the time they got through the line to greet Crunch, then made their way into the arena itself to find their seats, the pregame festivities had reached a crescendo. Val settled into one of their three hard plastic chairs, with Dev on the other end and Cam sandwiched between them. Several people around them nodded and smiled, one lady cooing about how cute Cam was.

"This place is packed," Dev said as he shrugged out of his jacket and scanned the crowd. "Is it always like this for games?"

"Yep." Val grinned as he inhaled the smell of popcorn and beer. He hadn't been to a game since the funeral, and he'd missed them. Vicki had been a die-hard Timberwolves fan, and he'd often come with her and Alex. But Alex had been too busy with his job recently and Val didn't like to come alone, so...

A vendor passed by, and Val stopped him to buy each of them a drink. The knot of tension that had been present since he'd gotten the text Thursday night was easing. This would be fine. They'd have a good time here, and maybe they could leave all that unresolved baggage that still lingered between them like an overloaded laundry line behind. No more awkwardness. That was Val's greatest wish at this point. It made everything harder, and he longed for the ease they'd once shared. And sure, Dev had to have some scars left behind from his divorce from douchebag Tom, but if they could just move past all that, it would be such a relief. And if they could somehow recover some semblance of their old friendship, that would be even better. With Vicki gone, no one knew his past better than Dev now, and vice versa. Dev knew about his deadbeat parents, and why Val was so outgoing was partly because he wanted people to like him. Because if people liked you, they treated you better. And he knew all about Dev's triggers too—the abandonment by his father, the misplaced shame and embarrassment of thinking that he was somehow responsible for his dad leaving. It had had nothing to do with Dev and everything to do with the man's own issues and selfishness. He'd missed being able to talk to Dev, knowing that Dev would understand when almost no one else would.

Before he could get too lost down that path though, the announcer thankfully drew him back to the here and now by asking everyone to stand for the national anthem.

Soon, the game got underway, and the roar of the crowd surged like a wave as the Timberwolves claimed possession, and Val and Cam got swept up in the collective excitement, jumping to their feet and cheering whenever their team scored. Dev remained seated, more reserved as always, clapping but not going overboard. Val had to chuckle. Even now, he'd never met anyone more in control of his emotions than Devon Harrison. It was one of the things that had drawn Val to the guy from the start and something he still admired, since he tended to be too emotional himself sometimes. Having grown up surrounded by such chaos, never knowing what he'd get at home from his alcoholic parents, Val found that being around Dev, who always came across as so calm and collected, had been a true revelation. Not that it wasn't challenging too sometimes, when he wished Dev could get upset more, but the only time that had ever happened was the night of the bachelor party when he'd told Dev about Tom…

Wincing slightly, he hazarded another glance Dev's way, hoping he hadn't noticed, but Dev seemed totally engrossed in the action on the court, his jaw shadowed by a hint of dark stubble that Val had a sudden urge to lean over and lick just to see what Dev would do and…

And what the…?

Stunned at himself, Val sat back and swallowed hard. Where the hell had that come from? He'd been telling the truth the other night when he'd told Alex that this was about friendship. That was all. He'd never wanted to cross that line with Dev, never wanted to push the well-established boundaries they'd set for themselves all those years ago, so why the hell was he suddenly having these thoughts now? The connection they'd had and lost, but might have again if he was careful, was too precious to risk the possibility of more.

Isn't it?

"Go! Go!" Cam shouted as the Timberwolves scored another basket against the opposing team, jarring Val out of those dangerous thoughts. No. He didn't want to get involved with Dev like that now. Sex made everything more complicated, and they already had enough issues between them to deal with.

Thinking about wanting Dev that way was stupid. Ridiculous. Absurd.

Then Dev glanced over at him and a fresh shot of kinetic attraction shot straight through

Val, making his knees wobble even though he was sitting down, and that's when he knew.

This was going to be a problem.

He had to hide it, had to keep it to himself until he could move past it. To that end, he stood and hoisted Cam onto his shoulders and moved down to the railing for a better view, and as applause erupted around them, he put as much distance as he could between himself and the man who suddenly filled him with a need that threatened everything Val had said he wanted. His heart felt like it would pound out of his chest. Maybe he was taking the coward's way out, but at least Dev would never know because he'd never tell him.

Unless he asks...

Because he'd also vowed after the fight they'd had that he'd always be truthful with Dev.

The guy deserved that after all the lies he'd been fed by his ex-husband.

But is the truth best about this?

Val was still pondering that conundrum as the first quarter closed and the buzzer blared. He took Cam to the restroom, waited in line there, then caught another vendor on the way back as the next quarter started to buy more drinks and popcorn. As they took their seats once more, Dev still sat there, looking at least a bit more relaxed than before, which was good. Not wanting to disturb that—and to cover his own inner turmoil over his newly discovered desire—Val tried making small talk, pointing down to where the players were currently huddled around their coach courtside during a time-out. "Quite the game, huh? Remember those charity matches we used to play during residency?"

"I do," Dev said, watching a replay of the last call on the overhead screen. "You always played a mean offense."

"Only because I knew your defense tactics by heart." Val snorted.

"True," Dev conceded. "You were always good at reading people, on and off the court."

"I try," he said, feeling some of the tension ease between his shoulder blades. Maybe it was just an isolated thing, that hot stab of want he'd felt toward Dev. It had been a long time since he'd gotten laid. Too long, probably. That had to be it. Yep. "That group of friends I mentioned from medical school still plays on the weekend sometimes. I'll let you know the next time we get together. We also play board games too. Trivial Pursuit, Pictionary, Cards Against Humanity. Though that last one can get kind of brutal. Hilarious, but brutal."

Dev chuckled. "I don't think you want to go against me at Trivial Pursuit. Did you know I once auditioned for *Jeopardy!* while I was living in California?"

"No way." Val straightened, forgetting all about his desire now as he learned this new important information. That had been their favorite show back in medical school. "How far did you make it?"

"All the way up to the in-person audition with the producers. I was so excited because I thought maybe I'd finally get to meet Alex Trebek, but then I messed up what should have been the easiest answer ever because of my nerves."

Val frowned. "What was it?"

"Who was the king of the Zulu Kingdom from 1816 to 1828?" He cringed. "I meant to say 'Who is Shaka Zulu?' But what came out instead was 'Who is Chaka Khan?'"

Val couldn't contain his laughter, especially when the DJ at the arena chose that moment to play Ms. Khan's eighties megahit "I Feel for You" after an impressive three-pointer by the home team. Soon Dev was laughing too, and it was like the years disappeared. Cam ignored them both, too enthralled with the game to pay either of them much attention. The moment lasted a few seconds before Dev returned to his usual contained self and focused on the game once more, but it was enough to confirm to Val that he'd made the right choice to ignore his new feelings toward Dev. That glimmer was enough to convince him that a return to their old connection might be possible after all.

The game continued with a spectacular score from a Timberwolves star player, causing the crowd to erupt into raucous cheers. Val gave it a standing ovation, grinning over at Dev, who was on his feet too, while Cam did a little victory dance between them. The Timberwolves were so far ahead now that it would be virtually impossible for the other team to win as the clock ticked down in the final quarter. The air felt electric as the last few seconds ticked down on the clock and the Timberwolves point guard launched one final shot. As the basketball arced as if in slow motion toward the basket, a hushed whisper took over the arena as every eye followed the ball. When it kissed the rim then fell through the net, the home crowd erupted in triumph. Val picked up Cam and put him on his shoulders again as elation surged between their trio. "Did you see that?"

"Yes!" Dev grinned, his usual reserve giving way to genuine awe. "Unbelievable!"

Eventually, the crowd began to dissipate, and they made their way out of the stadium. Val's arm occasionally brushed Dev's as they weaved through people, sending forbidden tingles through him before he shoved them down. Cam couldn't stop talking about the game and the kid was practically floating with energy now. Val was glad the next day was Sunday, since he'd bet good money his son wouldn't fall asleep for a while, and there was no way he'd get up for school.

They reached Dev's car first. They stopped at the rear bumper to part ways. "Tonight was fun. Thanks for inviting me."

"Thanks for accepting," Val said, meaning it. "I'm glad you enjoyed it, and I hope it won't be the last time."

Dev nodded then stared down at the keys in his hand. "My mom thinks you can help me get out more."

"She's right." Val rocked back on his heels. "I'm happy to show you around again, if you want."

"We'll see," Dev said noncommittally, then transferred his attention to Cam. "How are you feeling?"

"I feel great!" Cam said, then yawned. "Good night, Dr. Dev."

Dev smiled, causing Val's heart to flip over before he scolded himself. "Good night, Cam."

Both men hesitated, one beat stretching into two, until finally Val picked up his son. "Well, I'll see you around the hospital, then."

"Yes, you will," Dev said. "We're still consulting together on Matt's case, since his results came back ALL and not mono. And let me know if you ever need me to check Cam again. Clinic or not."

"Will do. Thanks." Val backed away, waiting until Dev had gotten in his car and started the engine, before turning toward his SUV parked down the same row. It was a generous offer on Dev's part, and one Val might take him up on, if needed. They could do this. He could do this. Put Dev firmly back in the friendship category and be happy about it. He'd get over this weird new desire and things would get back to normal between them. He'd have the connection he wanted back in his life.

And maybe, if he told himself that enough times, he'd believe his own nonsense.

CHAPTER FOUR

WHEN HE'D OFFERED to check Cam again if needed, he'd hadn't expected a text from Val so soon. But here he was, parked outside of Val's house this time, ready to go in for what Val had called a "final check." Of course he'd said yes, because he considered Cam one of his patients now and because, well, he'd missed the boy. Missed Val too, if he was honest, even though it had only been a few days since the game.

Dev had never allowed himself to need a lot of other people around, so it was odd, honestly, missing them. Usually, he enjoyed his alone time. Even with Tom, he hadn't questioned how little time they had spent together because of their crazy schedules. In hindsight, maybe if he'd paid more attention then, he would've saved himself a lot of heartache.

Scowling, he got out and grabbed his medical bag, then walked up to the porch to ring the doorbell, ignoring the sudden thrumming of his heart against his ribs and nerves sizzling through him. Then the door opened to reveal a dark-haired woman with a kind smile.

"You must be Dr. Harrison," she said, holding out her hand. "I'm Nancy, the nanny. Please come in." She gestured him inside then took his coat. "I'll let Val and Cam know you're here. The kid hasn't stopped talking about that game. He's really taken a shine to you."

"I've taken a shine to him too," Dev said before she disappeared down the hall. While he waited, he sat on the sofa and glanced at several completed Lego structures stuck amidst the books on the built-in shelves along the walls, and the various colorful drawings strewn across the coffee table in front of him. He'd received his fair share of pictures from his patients over the years, so he considered himself a pretty good judge of talent, and Cam's were good.

Once upon a time, a home like this was all young Dev had dreamed of. Not that his mom hadn't done her best, but she'd had to work two jobs to keep a roof over their heads, and there was many a night when Dev had been left to his own devices. He hadn't thought about that in years, his loneliness back then, but being here reignited the pull of those old cravings for companionship. Except now he knew the price of letting someone that close and how badly you could get burned if you were wrong.

Before he could get too mired in the past, however, Cam raced into the living room in his stockinged feet, his blue eyes bright with excitement, looking about as healthy as a kid could get. "Dr. Dev! You're here!"

"I am," Dev said, his own smile matching the boy's enthusiasm. "Your dad asked me to come by."

"Cool!" He scrambled up onto the sofa next to Dev. "Did you save any kids today?"

Dev chuckled as he pulled on a pair of gloves from the medical kit. "Well, I met a little girl who loves dinosaurs as much as you love Lego." He held a digital thermometer against Cam's forehead. Ninety-eight point six. "We talked about triceratops while I gave her the medicine she needed."

"So you're a dino doc too?" Cam's eyes widened as Dev checked his pulse and respirations, then listened to the boy's lungs with his stethoscope. "That's so amazing!"

"Talking to her was pretty awesome," Dev agreed as he finished rechecking Cam's ears and throat. All clear. "Did you know that when I was your age, I wanted to be a paleontologist?"

"A pale what?" Cam scrunched his nose. "I don't know what that is."

"Paleontologist. They study dinosaurs for a living," he told the boy as he palpated the lymph nodes in Cam's neck and found them slightly swollen, but nothing unexpected after recovering from a cold as Cam had. They should be back to normal soon enough. "Did you know I used to dig in my backyard when I was your age, hoping I'd find a dinosaur bone?"

Cam gaped. "Did you ever find one?"

"No," Dev sighed, pulling off his gloves and returning them to his bag along with the rest of his stuff. "All I ever found were some plain old rocks, but I pretended they were fossils. My poor mom went along with it too to keep me happy. She used to say it was all about imagination."

"Uncle Val says that too!" Cam said, his gaze intent.

"What do I say?" Val asked, emerging from the hallway. "Sorry I was delayed—had to deal with a call from the ER. What did I miss?"

"That life is about imagination," Dev said, smiling at Cam. "We were just discussing dinosaurs."

"Dr. Dev said he dug in his backyard when

he was my age. Can I do that too, Uncle Val? Please?"

"Uh…no." Val shook his head and walked over to sit in an armchair across from them, looking far too relaxed and delectable for his own good. Not that Dev noticed. Nope. "I think you have more than enough hobbies to keep you busy right now, don't you? Between Lego and soccer and drawing and Star Wars?"

"I guess," Cam sighed, then jumped off the couch. "Wait here, Dr. Dev. I'm gonna get the new Lego toy I built to show you."

He sprinted off down the hall again, leaving Val and Dev alone in the living room.

"I examined him as well, while we talked, and he's one hundred percent healthy. As if his energy wasn't enough of a sign," Dev said.

"Good, thanks." Val sat forward. "I got that humidifier you recommended too, and it seems to help."

"Excellent. Glad to hear it."

"I'm leaving for the night," Nancy said, re-appearing with her coat on and her purse over her shoulder. "Unless you need anything else, Val. Nice to meet you, Dr. Harrison."

"You too," Dev said. "And please, call me Dev."

"Good night, Nancy. Thanks for everything."

"Sure thing." She gave them a little wave. "See you in the morning."

After she left, the ensuing moments stretched taut and the silence grew uncomfortable. Dev finally stood. "Well, I should probably get going then too. Unless you need something else from me."

"Dr. Dev! Look at this!" Cam ran back in and thrust an oddly shaped blue building up at him. "Isn't it cool?"

"It sure is," Dev said, doing his best to look suitably impressed, even though he had no clue what the thing was. "It's very…blue."

"It's Stark Tower," Val supplied helpfully, humor edging his tone. "You know, from *The Avengers*."

"Oh, right." Dev nodded, shooting Val a grateful glance. That movie was from a while ago, so it had slipped his mind. "I loved *The Avengers*."

"Me too," Cam said. "I'm gonna be Iron Man one day."

"Really?" Dev crouched to put himself and Cam at eye level. "You have to be really brave for that."

"I can be brave, Dr. Dev!" Cam placed his hands on his hips in a superhero pose. "See?"

"I do see," Dev agreed, straightening and ruffling the boy's hair. "Very brave indeed."

"You're brave too, Dr. Dev," Cam continued, patting Dev's hand. "Saving people."

Considering how his life had gone the past few years, brave wasn't a word Dev would've used about himself. But now, looking back, maybe it had taken some courage to walk away from the life he'd planned with Tom in California and return to Minneapolis. At the time, he'd just wanted to get as far away as possible from all that pain, but perhaps some small part of him had also sought the comfort of the only place that had ever felt like home. He managed to say, "Thank you, Cam. That means a lot."

Thankfully, if Val noticed the crack in Dev's voice at those words, he didn't mention it.

Lord, what was happening to him? He'd gone from feeling nothing to nearly crying when a kid paid him a compliment. Maybe he was more tired after a long day than he'd thought.

Cam clambered back down the hall again, presumably to grab more toys for Dev to admire, and Val clapped Dev on the shoulder, making him jump. He hadn't even seen Val move because he'd been so focused on the boy.

"He'll keep you here all night showing you his stuff, if you're not careful," Val said, chuckling as he headed for the open kitchen behind them. "He's got a ton of Lego."

"Oh, well," Dev said, grabbing his medical bag, more flustered from that brief touch than he cared to admit. "I guess I'd better get going then."

Before he made it back to the foyer, where Nancy had hung his coat earlier, Cam was back. This time with a toy Dev recognized. "I finished my Microfighter too! See?"

"Oh, wow, Cam!" This time Dev didn't have to pretend to be impressed. It was a complicated and difficult build and Cam had done it in just a few days, apparently. The last time he'd heard the boy talk about it, he'd just started the new set. He took the model gently from Cam's hands to admire it up close. "This is amazing."

"Thanks. I can't wait to take it to school tomorrow and show my friends. I have lots of friends," Cam said, looking proud of himself. "My mom always said I could make friends with a tree."

"You take after your uncle." Dev grinned, glancing over at Val, who was watching them from behind the island. "Being sociable can be a good thing though. Helps you meet new people and learn new things. You can adapt easily and make life an adventure."

"Yes! I love adventures." Cam grinned over at Dev before growing serious again. "Did you have a lot of friends growing up, Dr. Dev?"

By now he should be used to children's astuteness. Back when he'd been doing his pediatric oncology fellowship, one of the first things his mentor had told him was to always be truthful with the children under his care, because they would see through a lie in a second. He'd always kept to that rule over the past eight years, and it had never steered him wrong. Tonight would be no exception, even though telling the truth left Dev feeling far more exposed than he'd like. He gave a curt shake of his head. "No. I wasn't as sociable as you, Cam," he answered honestly. "I did have this stuffed bear I'd take everywhere with me when I was your age. He was like a friend who never left my side."

"I never knew you had a bear," Val said quietly from the kitchen. Dev didn't dare risk a glance at him, afraid those sturdy walls he'd built around himself might take another hit.

"Did your bear have a name?" Cam asked.

Dev's answer sounded gruffer than intended. "Sir Bearington."

"Like Mr. Trunks!" Cam said, rushing to a corner of the living room to pick up a well-loved elephant plushie. "Before I started school all day, he went everywhere with me. Now he stays home." Unexpected warmth spread through Dev's chest, and he resisted the urge to rub the area over his heart. "Sometimes I still talk to him about stuff though…like how I miss my mom, or how I worry about Uncle Val working too hard."

"That's good. Talking helps," Dev agreed, thinking back to the long nights he'd spent confiding in his own stuffed bear. "After my father left, I used to talk to Sir Bearington about things too, like how I felt lonely."

Val came back into the living room to crouch beside Cam, looking concerned, and Dev's pulse took another tumble before he stepped back, away from temptation.

"You think I work too much, buddy?" Val asked. "I don't want you worrying about me."

Cam shrugged, setting the plushie aside. "I just don't want to lose you like I lost my mom."

"Oh, Cam," Val said, pulling his son into a hug. "You know I'll never leave you if I can help it."

Things had gotten very emotional very fast, and Dev felt adrift in a treacherous sea that could easily overwhelm him. He needed to get out of here now before he did something silly like end up in a huddle hug with Val and Cam…

or just Val. And the thought of being that close to Val, pressed against him, feeling his heat, surrounded by his clean, citrusy scent, was too much. He cleared his throat and turned back toward the door again. "I'm going to go now."

Val glanced at him from over the top of Cam's head and frowned. "Please stay for dinner. It's the least I can do to repay you making another trip over here."

"Yes, Dr. Dev!" Cam chimed in, racing over to grab Dev's hand. "Please stay for dinner!"

"Oh, I don't think—" Damn. He didn't want to disappoint Cam. And with things between him and Val finally approaching something close to normal, he didn't want to backslide into the frozen tundra their relationship had been before the basketball game by insulting him. And, well, he hadn't eaten all day, and the smells now drifting from the kitchen from whatever Val had put in the oven smelled delicious. Besides, he was a grown adult. He could get through one dinner with Val without revealing his troublesome feelings to him. Lord knew he'd become a master of hiding his emotions over the years. He could do it again here. "Well, if you both insist. Thank you. Dinner sounds great."

"Awesome!" Cam clapped and jumped around, as if this was the best news ever.

"The lasagna has about five more minutes to reheat," Val said, checking the oven again. "Cam, can you set the table, please?"

While the boy did as he was asked, with a stack of mismatched plates and silverware that Val had handed him, Dev stood there wondering what to do with himself. So, he took a seat at the table and waited until the oven timer went off. Cam soon climbed onto the chair across from him as Val carried in a steaming pan of what looked like Vicki's old homemade lasagna recipe. He dished up generous portions for each of them, the aroma of tomato sauce and garlic and baked cheese making Dev's stomach growl. He hadn't eaten since grabbing a quick energy bar for breakfast at his mother's house that morning. Val returned to the kitchen for a basket of breadsticks, then sat down as well.

While they ate, Cam kept up the conversation. "Did you save any lives today, Uncle Val?"

"Don't talk with your mouth full, buddy," Val chided him gently, undermining it a bit by laughing. "And no. Today was just the usual ER stuff. Broken arms and cuts and bruises. What about you, Cam? Any superhero feats in school today? How'd your test go?"

They chatted about their days as Dev nearly died from food ecstasy. He'd forgotten how good this recipe of Vicki's was and ended up stuffing himself full of carbs, which was good because it left little room for all the confusing emotions he'd been dealing with earlier. By the time they finished eating and cleaning up, and Val sent Cam to his room to get ready for bed, things almost felt comfortable.

Dev took this as the perfect time to leave before things got sticky again. "Thank you again for dinner."

This time, Val didn't stop him, following him to the door instead, a sheepish grin on his face. "I'd invite you to stay longer, but I owe Cam story time before he'll go to sleep, which can take a while depending on the book, so…"

And damn if Dev's throat didn't tighten with yearning over picturing Val and Cam snuggled in bed, cozy and secure.

What the hell is happening to me?

He'd never had an issue keeping his walls high and strong, but the more time he spent with these two, the more difficulty he was having keeping them in place. It was terrifying and thrilling all at once.

Val reached past Dev to open the door, putting them even closer. "Thank you for coming by to check on Cam again, and putting an overprotective new dad's mind at ease. I really appreciate it, Dev."

Their eyes met then, and as if drawn inexplicably by some invisible cord, Dev found himself leaning toward Val. He wasn't sure what he intended to do, maybe hug him or clap him on the shoulder as Val had done to him earlier, but then something changed in the air between them. Something charged and sparkling, volatile and electric. As if in a daze, he whispered, "Cam's lucky to have you."

"We're lucky to have each other," Val replied, his voice equally low and sincere as his gaze flicked to Dev's lips before returning to his eyes again. "He's become my anchor."

And in that moment, Dev couldn't have moved if he'd tried. He was held in place by the craving inside him to kiss Val, even as the shadows of old fears urged him to run far and fast from the feelings that could destroy everything he'd thought he'd wanted.

Blood pounded through his body with the force of a drum. They both had so much to lose if they crossed this line—Dev's new life and career and Val's role as Cam's sole parent. Neither of them could afford to screw those things up.

Go. Now. Before it's too late.

Somehow, Dev found the strength to break the spell woven around them and hurried outside, his breath rough from the dance of desire and trepidation twirling through his body, leaving him dizzy. He fumbled his steps, stumbling over his words. "I… I'm sorry… I really need to go."

Val blinked at him, looking as confused as Dev felt as he fled into the night. What had almost happened there was a mistake. An aberration. And it couldn't happen again. Dev couldn't allow it to happen again. Because he'd been down that impetuous road before, letting his emotions rule over his head, only to discover too late he'd been wrong.

He wouldn't make the same mistake again.

The answer was simple. Get some space and distance and it would all go away.

CHAPTER FIVE

IT DIDN'T GO AWAY.

In fact, the more he tried not to think about Val and what had occurred between them at that doorway, the more he couldn't stop those thoughts from flooding back. Over the past two days, he'd replayed every second of that almost-kiss, over and over, desperate to understand why it had happened, and most importantly, how to ensure it didn't happen again. Because he and Val were finally back on cordial terms again and he didn't want to ruin that by bringing anything more complicated into that mix. And if he woke up at night, hot and sweaty, blood thrumming, well, that was his problem to deal with—in an icy cold shower.

And deal with it he did, because it wasn't like they could avoid each other. They had to work certain cases together, like Matt Warden's. Which is what had Dev worked up this morning. Not that things had taken a turn for the worse with their young patient. On the contrary, all the test results showed that Matt was responding well to treatment and making steady, gradual improvement with his leukemia. No. It was the fact that Matt and his mother were coming in for a follow-up that morning and it would be the first time Dev saw Val after the night at his house.

He'd come in early for his shift after a sleepless night, and now sat in his office in the oncology department, nursing a cup of strong coffee. He already felt wired enough from nerves to power the entire state of Minnesota, and was staring at a lab report he'd already memorized of the results for Matt without really seeing it, because his mind continued to churn with anxiety over how he'd handle seeing Val again. His current mood hovered between dejected and determined.

Determined to stay professional and on track during the follow-up, because Matt and his mother deserved his very best care and that's what they'd get from him. Dejected, because he couldn't understand why he failed to control his emotions where Val was concerned. He'd tried everything he could think of to jar himself out of it—remembering the worst few weeks after the breakup of his marriage, when he'd felt lost

and adrift in a sea of hurt and self-recriminations; when he'd sworn never to end up there
again in his life, no matter what it took—but
nothing seemed to do the trick.

It was maddening. It was alarming. It was
also oddly energizing, challenging him to do
better.

And Dev had always relished a challenge.

And speaking of challenges, a glance as his
smartwatch said it was time for the consult with
Matt and his mother.

With a sigh, Dev closed the laptop on his desk
and stood, smoothing a hand down the front of
his pristine white lab coat before heading out of
his office and down the hall that led to the busy
nurses' station out front. Shoulders squared,
he reminded himself of his professional duty,
his years of practice and his expertise. He'd remain aloof and focused, and everything would
be fine. Chances were good that Val wouldn't
even remember their encounter by the door that
night. Just because Dev couldn't seem to get it
out of his mind didn't mean Val was fixated
on it too...

Gah. I'm being ridiculous.

Frustrated with his own inability to get past
this, Dev grabbed his tablet and headed for
Matt's room. Val was mostly likely already

in there, so hopefully they could get this done quickly. As he opened the consultation room door, Dev flashed his most professional smile at Matt and his mother. "Good morning, Matt. Ms. Warden." He hazarded a brief glance at Val, who stood off to the side, arms crossed, stretching the blue scrubs he wore enticingly over the muscled torso beneath. Dev swallowed hard and diverted his attention fast to the screen of the tablet in his hand, mumbling, "Dr. Laurent."

Dev took a seat on a stool across from the patient and his mother, and got down to business. "Well, the good news is that your white blood count is coming up, Matt, which is exactly what we want to see after this initial round of chemo. We still have a way to go, but things are headed in the right direction for now."

Val nodded. "Dr. Harrison is right. I had a look at your results down in the ER myself and you're doing great, Matt. And you're in the best hands for care. Keep fighting, and we'll have you back playing with your team before you know it."

"Thanks." Matt flashed a tired smile beneath the blue knit cap that covered his balding scalp. "That's really great news."

After a brief chat to discuss treatment plans going forward, answer questions and recommend several natural supplements to help Matt with energy and brain fog, Dev shook their hands then headed back to his office to dictate his notes from the consult, using the new secure app on his phone the hospital was trying out with the physicians on staff. But before he could start, the phone buzzed in his hand and his mother's face popped up on the caller ID. He took a seat behind his desk and answered.

"Mom, everything okay?" he asked, concerned.

"Everything's fine, honey. I just wanted to remind you to stop at the store on your way home and pick up the basil I need for dinner tonight," she said. "Maybe another bottle of white wine too, since I'll use up what I have in the recipe."

Dev leaned back in his chair and took off his glasses, then massaged the bridge of his nose between his thumb and forefinger, eyes closed. Now that the nervous energy he'd been running on prior to seeing Val again was gone, his lack of sleep was catching up with him. He yawned, then said, "I won't forget, Mom."

"Is that Elaine?" Val asked from the doorway, making Dev bolt up in his seat and nearly drop his phone on the floor.

"Uh…" he said, shoving his glasses back on, glad for the desk between them as a smiling Val stepped into the office and seemed to take up all the space available. "Yes."

"Who are you talking to, honey?" his mother said from the other end of the line. "Is that Val?"

Crap.

"Tell her I said hello," Val said, sitting down in one of the chairs across from Val, looking far too relaxed for Dev's comfort. Was he really oblivious to the sizzling chemistry between them that was driving Dev nuts? Apparently. When Dev didn't respond, Val called, "Hi, Elaine!"

"Honey, put me on speaker so I can talk to him," his mom said.

Reluctantly, Dev did as she asked, wondering who exactly in the universe he'd annoyed that they seemed to be conspiring against him now. He set the phone on his desk and Val leaned forward, his grin widening. "It's so good to hear your voice again, Elaine. How are you?"

"I'm good, Val. How are you? Still holding in there?" His mother's tone turned concerned. "How's poor Cam?"

"Cam is great, thanks for asking. We're doing okay. It's an adjustment but were getting through it. Also thank you for the flowers at Vicki's funeral. I never got a chance to say that personally and I'm sorry. Things were so crazy there for a while."

"No worries at all."

While they chatted, Dev turned his attention on sorting through his email on his laptop and ignoring the fact that with Val so close, he could catch the scent of soap and clean, warm maleness from his skin. Which only made the unwanted, simmering need low in his gut kick up a notch closer to full boil.

Enough.

He finally picked up his phone again, intent on ending this torture. "Right. If you two are caught up, I do have other work I need to attend to. Mom, I will pick up the things you need at the store and see you tonight when I get home."

"Val, I'm making chicken cacciatore, your favorite," his mother said before Dev could shut off the speakerphone. "Why don't you and Cam come over and join us if you don't have other plans? I'd love to meet Cam and see you again, and you can both get a good home-cooked meal."

"I'd love that, Elaine," Val said, grinning over at Dev. "What time should we be there? And can I bring anything?"

"Seven, and just yourselves," Elaine said. "Can't wait to see you both then."

"Same. Thanks again." Val sat back at last as Dev ended the call before fate could taunt him anymore. Val's grin slowly faded as he looked at Dev. "I hope it's okay that we come. If you don't want me to, I won't."

Great. Now Dev was stuck between a rock and a hard place. If he said no, that it was fine, he'd have to endure a whole night of sitting beside Val, thinking about their almost-kiss and how that could never ever happen again. If he said yes, then that made him sound petty and mean. And he would like to see Cam again. The kid was like a walking, talking ray of sunshine.

In the end, there wasn't much of a choice. "It's fine," he said curtly. "Now, if you'll excuse me, I really do have work to do."

"Sure." Val stood and walked back to the door, stopping there to look back at Dev. "Listen, about the other night…"

Oh, boy.

Dev squeezed his eyes shut and took a deep breath, fearful that Val would read too much in his eyes. "What about it?" he said, hoping to sound as detached as possible. "We had a nice dinner and some conversation. That's it."

Val just stood there, the weight of his stare heavy on the side of Dev's head. "Seriously?"

Exasperated and feeling trapped, Dev finally opened his eyes and threw up his hand as he looked at Val. "What? What do you want me to say? That we almost kissed by the door?" With the door open, he made sure to keep his voice low enough that his personal life wouldn't become fodder for the hospital gossip mill. "It was a mistake. I'm sorry. I don't know what I was thinking. Let's just forget all about it, all right?"

At that moment, Dev wished for nothing more than for a hole to open beneath him and swallow him completely—at least then, he could escape the embarrassing shame spiral he now found himself in.

Instead of leaving, Val stepped into the office and closed the door behind him, causing Dev's already-racing heart to triple its speed. "Dev, forgetting about it won't help. We can work through this."

Dev snorted. Sure. He knew firsthand it wouldn't be that easy. "I don't have time for this right now."

Val blinked at him. "Like I do?" He shook his head, hands on hips as he stared down at the floor. "Look, we might not know each other that well now, but you were the closest friend I had for years, and I'd bet good money you've been overanalyzing everything since that night."

Dev resented the fact that he was right. "I'm not sure what that has to do with this…weird thing…between us."

"It's not weird, it's attraction. And it's normal." Val watched him closely for a beat or two, then sighed. "Doesn't mean we have to act on it, okay? I just want things to be good between us again. Cam really likes you, and I don't want him hurt in all this because we decided to do something foolish."

"I like Cam too. He's a great kid." Forcing himself to breathe, Dev swallowed the lump in his throat. "And I don't want him hurt either. So, like I said, we forget all about the other night and move on like it never happened. Agreed?"

"Agreed. I need to get back downstairs. The ER was slammed when I left." Val opened the door and stepped out into the hallway again, sending Dev a last dazzling smile over his shoulder. "See you at seven."

Dev just sat there for a full minute after he left, wondering how the hell he'd ended up here in the first place—and more importantly, how he was going to get through the night ahead without getting close to Val to keep his sanity. They'd agreed, after all, and Dev knew then he was in big, big trouble.

After his shift, Val ran home, showered and changed, then stood before the mirror in his bedroom, adjusting the collar of his white dress shirt for the umpteenth time. The expression staring back at him looked more like a man gearing up for battle than one preparing for a casual dinner at a friend's house. Which was ridiculous. This was dinner with Elaine and Dev. Back in the day, he'd gone over to their house a couple of times a week for study sessions or just to hang out. It wasn't a big deal.

Except it sure felt like it was.

Despite the agreement he and Dev had reached in his office to not pursue things between them.

Because he knew he hadn't misread things the other night in the foyer. That if he'd just leaned in a little more, he and Dev would've kissed, and Val would've loved it. At first, his reaction when thinking about kissing Dev had taken Val by surprise, but he'd since come to terms with the fact that he wanted Dev as more than a friend now. Maybe it was a side effect of losing him for so long after the wedding, then getting him back unexpectedly, but this felt like a second chance and Val knew how rare those were. He didn't want to let this one slip through his fingers. And if Dev only wanted to be friends, that was fine. He'd deal with it. He'd take whatever he could get with Dev, honestly. For so long, he'd feared their cherished connection had disappeared forever, so an opportunity to revive it now sounded like the best idea in the world to Val, however that looked for them. It would be fine. Val would make sure of it. For himself and for his son too, since Cam had taken to Dev so quickly.

Just keep yourself grounded and take it slow.

He took a deep breath and gave up on studying his own reflection. He walked down the hall to Cam's room instead to make sure he was ready to go. Cam had insisted on wearing his new Timberwolves jersey, the one they'd bought for the game, despite the fact it was too big for him. He'd barely taken it off all week, so rather than argue, Val let him. Picking your battles was an essential rule of parenthood.

"Do you think Dr. Dev will let me see his models?" Cam asked as Val made sure the kid's sneakers were tied. "Did they even have Lego when he was a kid?"

Val bit back a laugh as he ruffled the boy's hair. "Yes, they had Lego back then. How old do you think Dev and I are?"

"Old." Cam tugged on his jacket as he raced for the front door.

The drive over to Elaine's house was uneventful, with Cam telling Val the whole way about his day at school. Val nodded or responded at the appropriate times, though his mind was only half on the conversation and half on seeing Dev again soon.

He'd meant what he'd said earlier, about wanting things to be good. And if that meant forgetting all about whatever this thing was that was developing between them, well, Val was okay with that too. Yes, he was attracted to Dev, but he would never act on it unless he got a clear signal from Dev that that's what he wanted too. And of course, there was Cam to consider as well. He didn't want to ruin the budding friendship between those two either, and if he and Dev did get involved, then it could get messy if it all went off the rails. Sex would only complicate that situation further.

When they finally pulled into the driveway, a jolt of nostalgia ran through Val. The ranch-style suburban home looked just as he remembered, with its warmly lit windows and manicured lawn. He and Cam got out and walked up to the front door, but before he could knock, the door swung open, and there was Elaine in her wheelchair, her kind eyes and gentle smile calming all Val's nerves.

"Valentine Laurent, it feels like forever since I've seen you," she exclaimed, pulling him down for a hug before turning her attention to

Cam. "And Cameron. It's so nice to meet you in person finally. I knew your mom well."

Cam tilted his head, studying her. "I remember the flowers you sent to the funeral. They were the biggest ones there."

Elaine hugged him too. "Precious boy."

She waited until they were inside before whispering to Val once Cam was busy searching for Dev. "I know my son is probably too stubborn to say this himself, but I'm really glad you two found each other again. I know he could use the support after everything that happened out in California, and I'm sure you could too, raising Cam on your own now. I think you both need each other."

"I'm glad too," he said, bending to kiss her cheek again. "And thank you for caring."

While she returned to the kitchen to check on dinner, Val took off his coat then grabbed Cam's from where he'd tossed it on the sofa, and hung them both up in the closet. There was no sign of Dev yet, and Val wondered where he was. Then Cam raced out of the kitchen, laughing, followed in short order by Dev, who was wiping his hands on a dish towel. He'd changed out of his office attire and now had on jeans and a sweater, looking sexier than anyone should be allowed to. He adjusted his glasses and raised a hand in greeting to Val. "Hi. Can I get you anything to drink? Dinner should be ready soon."

"Water would be great, thanks," Val said past his dry throat. Dev seemed more relaxed now that he was home, his normally neatly combed hair slightly ruffled and his cheeks flushed from cooking at the stove. The scent of tomato sauce and cooked chicken had Val's stomach rumbling. He hadn't eaten all day because the ER had been slammed again. Then his eyes locked with Dev's and a hunger of an entirely different kind took over.

Whoa there, cowboy.

He needed to remember their agreement. This was just dinner amongst friends, nothing more. And the sooner his libido got that memo, the better, because right now, all he could imagine was walking over there and diving his fingers into Dev's dark hair and finishing that kiss they'd almost started the other night, witnesses and agreements be damned. And that was a problem.

Thankfully, Cam interrupted, basically throwing ice water over the heat threatening to become a wildfire in Val's blood by asking, "Dr. Dev, can I see your models?"

"Sure," Dev said, tearing his eyes away from

Val and tossing the dish towel on the table. "A few of them are still in the den. This way."

"Cool!" Cam said, skipping beside Dev down the hall.

"Here's that water you asked for," Elaine said, returning to the living room.

Val thanked her, then sank onto one end of the sofa and took a much-needed breath. Maybe keeping to that agreement wouldn't be as easy as he'd thought, based on his reactions just now.

"So, tell me what you've been up to lately?" She parked her wheelchair beside an armchair perpendicular to him and smiled. "Chicken still has about five more minutes before it's done."

"Not much, other than working," Val said, some of the tension inside him dissipating. "The ER really doesn't have a downtime. People are always getting injured somehow. What about you?"

They chatted about her church group and bridge club, then moved on to Cam's school activities. Finally, Elaine circled back to him and Dev again. "I'm so glad you're here tonight, Val. Dev's kept himself so isolated since the separation and divorce. He could really use a friend like you right now, even if he'd never say it himself."

Val took another sip of his water to dislodge

the lump that had formed there at the thought of Dev being so lonely. "I'm sure he'll settle in and make new friends here."

Elaine gave him a look. "Now, you know as well as I do that my son isn't good with people, outside of his patients. He's not a social butterfly like you." She shrugged. "My hope is coming home can be a new start for him, and I think regaining that close friendship with you might be the beginning he needs."

Dev returned then, sans Cam, and took a seat on the other end of the sofa from Val. "He's busy checking out my old models. That'll keep him occupied for a while." He flashed Val a shy smile that set his traitorous heart racing again.

"I'll go check on that chicken again. Should be close to done by now," Elaine said, excusing herself, leaving him and Dev alone in the living room.

"The house looks the same," Val said, feeling tongue-tied for the first time in recent memory. Man, he was nervous, like a blind date before prom. Then Dev started fiddling with his glasses, a familiar sign that he was nervous too, and that knowledge put Val a bit more at ease. "It's good to be back here. Lots of great memories."

Dev huffed out a breath. "I didn't want you here."

Val looked over at him, speechless. "Why?"

"You know why." Dev sat forward and hung his head, hands dangling between his knees. "I can't get involved with anyone again, I'm sorry. But if that's what you want, I need to be clear about that upfront, Val."

"That's why we have an agreement," Val said, confused. "You know you can trust me to keep it."

"That's the problem though." Dev gave an unpleasant laugh. "Trust. I don't trust anyone anymore. Not even myself. And it's my fault. I should have listened to you back then." His tone turned weary as he met Val's gaze, his dark eyes fathomless behind his glasses. "My biggest regret now is that I didn't. I could have saved everyone a lot of heartache. But instead, I blamed you and ignored the warning signs right in front of me. You were right and I was wrong. And it makes it harder because I'm torn between this unwanted attraction to you and the fact you're also a constant reminder of my own failures."

Stunned by this new information, Val scooted closer to him, wanting so badly to touch him, but knowing it would be unwelcome, even as a gesture of comfort. "Dev, I'm sorry about how things went down with us after the bachelor party, but we were both doing what we thought was right at that point with the information we had. You can't blame yourself for that. You were in love. Love makes people do crazy things, against their better judgment. And sometimes those choices don't work out, but it doesn't mean they're a failure. Especially if you learned something from it." Val huffed out a breath, staring down at his hands in his lap. "And if we're taking blame here, I could have done better too. The way I told you about what had happened at the party that night was so abrupt because I was angry on your behalf that Tom would've tried that with me, knowing you were my best friend, knowing I would tell you…" He shook his head and told him something he'd never spoken out loud before. "It was almost like Tom wanted me to tell you, like maybe he wanted to get out of the wedding but didn't know how, and I was scared for you. I knew how deeply you were invested in a future with him, so that fear spilled over into our argument too. But a day hasn't gone by since then that I don't wish we could go back and change it."

One silent beat stretched into two as those

painful memories filled Val's mind, crowding out everything else until he reminded himself that things were different now. They could make them different, if they both wanted to. "We have a second chance here, Dev. To start over, to start fresh. To leave the past behind and move forward as friends. Maybe not the same as before, but just as good. Is that what you want?"

Dev hesitated before shaking his head and scrubbing his hands over his face. "I don't know what I want anymore."

"Dinner's almost ready," Elaine called from the kitchen, and before Val could respond, Dev was up and walking away again. "I need to help her get things on the table."

Val watched him go, worried he'd said the wrong thing. Again. To distract himself, he picked up a photo album off the coffee table in front of him and flipped through it, looking at pictures of a young Dev—probably around Cam's age, if he had to guess—laughing, his messy hair covered in mud. He wished that his Dev of today could get some of that carefree exuberance back again, then stopped short.

My Dev?

Restless, he put the album down. Okay, looking at those photos wasn't the distraction he wanted. He got up and went to fetch Cam for dinner.

Soon, they all sat around the dining room table, piles of hearty chicken cacciatore over pasta filling their plates. Everyone dug into the delicious food while Cam answered Elaine's questions between bites.

"So, what things do you like to do after school, Cam?" she asked.

"Well, besides Lego, I like soccer." Cam's face lit up. "I scored two goals last game!"

"Fantastic!" Elaine exclaimed, matching his son's enthusiasm.

Val and Dev shared fleeting glances across the table, Dev's statement from earlier lingering between them like a dark scowl. Did Dev really not know what he wanted? That seemed hard to believe, given how logical and decisive he'd always been. No. What Val suspected was more likely that Dev knew exactly what he wanted; he just didn't want to want it.

Does he want me?

"Can we go white water rafting, Uncle Val?" Cam asked, jolting him out of his thoughts. "Please?"

"Oh. Uh…maybe? When you're big enough," Val said, trying to pick up the thread of conversation he'd dropped completely. "Why would you ask about that, buddy?"

"I saw it on a TV show last week and it looked so cool!" Cam said.

"Maybe you can go next summer," Elaine offered. "When you're a little bigger, if your Uncle Val says it's okay."

"Yes! I'd love that!" Cam bounced in his seat. "I hope I grow ten feet by then!"

"I don't, buddy. I'm going bankrupt keeping you in clothes as it is."

That even got a bit of a laugh out of Dev, and some of the stress sizzling in the air between them cleared. If only they could get back to being this easy again. The rest of dinner passed without consequence, and soon they were all stuffed and staring at empty plates.

"Thank you for dinner, Elaine," Val said. "It was delicious as always."

He nudged Cam's foot under the table. "Yes, thanks, Ms. Harrison. It was so good!"

"Glad you both enjoyed it," she said, pushing away from the table. "I hope you both won't be strangers from now on. And Cam, I'll try to make it to one of your soccer games soon. Now, if my son and new houseguest would like to earn his keep by clearing the table, that would be great."

"I'd love for you to come to my games!" Cam got up and ran around the table to hug Elaine while Val helped Dev carry the dirty dishes to the kitchen. Dev then washed while Val dried, a welcome lull in talking between them as they worked. By the time it was all cleaned up, it was time to go.

Val walked out into the living to find Cam and Elaine going through the same photo album he'd been looking at earlier. "Okay, buddy. Go get your jacket on. It's past your bedtime."

After putting on his own coat, Val hugged Elaine again at the front door and thanked her for inviting them, just as Cam returned and Dev emerged from the kitchen at last, looking troubled and uncertain. Val wanted to hug him too, but knew that wasn't allowed.

"Uncle Val, can I go with Elaine to see her garden gnome before we leave?" Cam asked, shuffling his feet. "She said he's really cool!"

"Uh…sure," Val said as Elaine winked at him. "As long as she doesn't mind."

"Not at all. Give you boys a chance to say your goodbyes." She opened the door and rolled out onto the front porch, followed closely by Cam. "We'll meet you at the car."

They disappeared down a paved path around the side of the house, leaving Dev and Val standing at the door alone again, just like the other night. Usually poised, Val wasn't sure what to do with his hands all of a sudden, where to look, what to say. He ended up with a lame "Well, good night, then."

"Good night," Dev murmured, still looking all dark and broody and so hot Val was surprised he wasn't scorched just from being in his vicinity.

Heart racing, Val tried to look anywhere but at Dev, but somehow his gaze ended up on Dev's mouth, his lips slightly parted as he took a hitched breath. Yeah, he needed to get out of here before he couldn't anymore. "I'll...uh... see you later then."

Val started to turn away, only to feel a hand on his arm, tugging him back around and into Dev's chest. Then Dev's mouth was on his, just a hesitant brush of lips, like a question asked and answered all at once, but everything else faded away. Their agreement. Their past. Their other responsibilities. Val wasn't sure what had changed between them, only that it had, and he couldn't regret it. Then Dev pulled back slightly, his stubble-covered jaw scraping against Val's skin. "I don't know why I did that."

Dev looked flushed and feral, his dark eyes sparkling with heat and hunger, and Val's fingers itched to dive into the man's perfect hair and muss him up a little more as he swayed toward Dev again. "I do."

Then they were kissing again, fiercer now, tasting, teasing, tempting…

"Uncle Val, I'm ready to go," Cam called from the side of the house as he and Elaine returned.

Val and Dev flew apart as reality crashed back down around them, the cold night air jarring after the fiery heat of their kiss.

Lips tingling, Val felt dizzy. He'd gotten so lost in the moment that he'd forgotten all about Cam. That had never happened. Never. He fumbled back a step or two, trying to sound normal and failing miserably as he stumbled over his words. "I…uh…we…uh…thanks again for dinner."

For his part, Dev looked equally flummoxed, clearing his throat to croak out, "Sure… Anytime…"

It felt like an eternity before he and Cam were back in the car and heading home, Val's pulse still jackhammering and his mind spinning. He wasn't sure exactly what that kiss had meant, just that Dev had initiated it, and Val had to figure out where to go from here, because their chemistry was off the charts and if it happened again, Val wasn't so sure they'd stop next time, agreement or not.

CHAPTER SIX

DEV SPENT ANOTHER sleepless night replaying
that kiss and was awake before dawn, staring
at the ceiling.

What the hell was I thinking?

The problem was he hadn't been thinking
at all. He'd allowed his emotions to take over
again, and now look at the mess he'd made. For
weeks now, he'd been doing his best to deny
the growing attraction between him and Val,
hoping it would just go away, but that kiss had
shown him that wasn't possible anymore, because the rational part of his brain had short-circuited when it came to Val, and now he couldn't
forget that kiss.

It had been good. Better than good. Better
than even his fantasies. Sweet and sexy and
hot with just the right hint of wicked. Dev had
sensed Val's surrender in that brief kiss too and
maybe that's what had got him in the end.

Or it was Val's smile? Or his sexy voice? Or…

He groaned and covered his face with his hands.

Somehow, without him knowing it, he'd become so lost in his need for Val that he wasn't sure how to find his way back again. Val had seemed right there with him, eager and willing. And if he was truthful with himself, that was what had ultimately pushed him over the edge and made him lose control.

And that loss scared him more than anything else.

Because this deep need boiling inside him for Val was unlike anything he'd ever experienced before, even with Tom. It had felt like home. But home had a way of lulling you into letting your guard down, then hitting you so hard your universe blew apart.

No. They needed to reestablish their agreement as they'd planned. Last night was an aberration. Eventually, things between him and Val would cool off again and they'd forget all about this pesky attraction that threatened everything he was working hard to rebuild in his life. Safety. Security.

Resolved, he got up, got ready, then headed into work early, his analytical mind continuing to churn through possible solutions and outcomes to the situation with Val as he drove on autopilot.

But about a block away from the medical center, sudden gridlock made him pay attention. Traffic that early in the morning was unusual, which meant there must be another cause for it. An accident, maybe?

After forty-five minutes of no movement at all, Dev decided to take matters into his own hands and check what was going on himself. Besides, if there was some type of medical emergency, it was his professional duty to help. He pulled over to the curb and parked, then shut off his engine and grabbed his medical bag from the back seat. He locked up the sedan before walking toward what looked like a scene of complete carnage about half a block away from the medical center entrance.

Red-and-blue emergency lights flashed atop the numerous squad cars, and there were multiple ambulances and emergency fire vehicles surrounding the wreckage of several piled-up cars. First responders and hospital personnel were on scene, darting between smoking piles of crumpled metal as the acrid scent of burning oil and rubber filled the air. Amidst the cacophony of sirens, the occasional pained scream of a trapped victim echoed.

From somewhere close by, he heard a familiar voice call, "Help! I need help over here!"

Val.

Heart in his throat, Dev dove into action, adrenaline coursing through his veins. Had Val been involved in this horrible event? God, he hoped not. He had to find him, make sure he was okay. He frantically scanned the faces of several rescued victims as he rushed deeper into the chaos. There had to have been at least six vehicles involved, maybe more. He looked for Val's SUV but couldn't see much past the haze of smoke that was growing denser around them. At least they were close to the hospital, so even the most critical patients could get treatment quickly if needed.

"Over here!" Val called again, snapping his attention to a vehicle on the far side of the scene, sandwiched between a large box truck and another compact car, the hood grotesquely twisted from the impact. An insidious hiss echoed from somewhere near the gas tank of the crushed vehicle, and it only fueled Dev's desperation to find Val. And what about Cam? Had he been involved too? Were they both trapped, unable to move, bleeding out? Dying?

Oh, God. Please let them be okay.

Then, as if on command, the smoke parted

enough for him to see a flash of blue scrubs standing on the other side of the crushed car, and his stomach went into freefall, especially as he got closer and saw the streaks of blood on Val's clothes. He broke into a run, dodging firemen and pieces of jagged metal, until he was standing on the sidewalk, staring down at a sweaty and grime-covered—but apparently unharmed—Val. No sign of the boy though. "What happened here? Where's Cam?"

Val swiped the back of a hand over his forehead, leaving a black streak of grease behind. "Cam's fine. He's home, getting ready for school with Nancy. I'm not sure what caused the accident, just that we all heard the commotion and rushed out to help anyway we could." He pointed to the crumpled vehicle beside them. "There's a woman trapped in there and they're going to have to cut her out."

"Help me, please!" the woman called from inside the wreckage.

"From what I can see, she's trapped by the steering column and the gas tank's leaking," Val said. "If they don't get her out soon, the whole thing could blow. I've been trying to flag one of the firefighters down but I'm not sure they can see me through all this smoke. Can you go get them and tell them what's going on here? Have them bring the Jaws of Life."

Dev set his medical bag on the sidewalk, then jogged back the way he'd come to find firefighters to help. By the time he'd flagged one down, who then got his superior involved as well, several minutes had passed before they got back. Dev found Val crouched near what was left of the vehicle's front bumper to peer inside the shattered passenger side window.

"Ma'am, my name is Dr. Laurent. I'm here to help you," Val called inside the crushed car to the trapped woman, his voice soothing despite the danger surrounding them. "The fire department will cut you out of here, but until then, keep talking to me, okay? Can you tell me your name?"

"Patty. My name's Patty," she panted.

"Nice to meet you, Patty. Can you tell me if you're hurt?"

"My right leg hurts."

"The firefighters are here, Val," Dev said, still trying to process what he was seeing. He'd chosen the slower pace of pediatric oncology for a reason. The immediacy of trauma was nonstop stress, but Val was calm like the eye of the storm.

"Can you move that leg, Patty?" Val asked. "Or is it trapped under something?"

Patty cried out again in agony. "No, I can't move it. I'm stuck. Please help me!"

"Doctors, you'll need to move back," one of the firemen said as a team moved in to stabilize the vehicle before they cut the woman out of it. "Wait over there, please."

He and Val stepped under a line of yellow tape blocking off the sidewalk nearby as the firefighters started up the Jaws of Life. The roar of its engine was like a chainsaw, and made it impossible to talk, but when Dev hazarded a glance at Val beside him, he found the same concern and relief he felt inside himself reflected back at him. It took several minutes for them to pry open even a partial section of the crushed vehicle. Enough for the firefighters to be able to see Patty's face and talk to her at least.

"Stay still, ma'am," one of the firefighters said as they peeled back another section of roof. "We'll have you out of there in a—"

The rest of his words were cut off by a loud screech as the wrecked vehicle tipped precariously despite the firefighters' best efforts, and Dev reached over and grasped Val's hand without thinking. Val squeezed Dev's fingers back as they both watched the race to free the woman from the car.

"Gas line's compromised," one of the firefighters called, just as the driver's side door finally came free. Paramedics quickly moved in and managed to get Patty out of the car and onto a bodyboard, then whisked her away to the ER before firefighters moved in with a huge hose to smother the entire vehicle with a flame-retardant foam to prevent an explosion.

By the time it was all over, Dev felt like he'd gone ten rounds with a heavyweight champion boxer. Val wasn't in much better shape, from the looks of him. As more hospital staff flooded the area to help the injured, they stood there, still holding hands. Neither of them ready to let go yet. When he'd left his mother's house this morning, Dev had intended to keep his distance from Val until he could be rational about the situation between them, but now he knew he had to face it head on.

Val finally looked down at himself and laughed. "Looks like I need to go back home and take another shower."

Dev nodded, staring down at their joined hands. "Looks like it."

"Either you're going to have to let me go—"

Val smiled "—or you're going to have to come with me."

"Oh," Dev said, snapping out of his daze, lost in Val's eyes. He let him go fast. "Sorry. I need to get up to my office to see patients. I have a full schedule today."

A hint of disappointment flashed across Val's face, so fast Dev would've missed it if he hadn't been paying such close attention. "Right. Sure. Um…maybe we could talk later?"

Dev's phone buzzed in his pocket and he pulled it out to see his practice's number on the screen, probably calling to find out where he was. "I need to take this. Text me and we'll set it up."

He grabbed his medical bag and headed inside, phone to his ear as he rode the elevator up to his floor. He'd go down later and move his car, but for now, he had patients waiting.

By the time he had enough time between appointments to take a break and check his messages, it was well into the afternoon. Val's shift ended at eight that night. He wanted to talk then.

Dev's first instinct was to say no, but he knew it was best to get this over with, so he told Val he'd meet him downstairs outside the ER entrance at eight fifteen.

The rest of his day passed in a blur of busyness and nervous tension, until finally Val found him waiting outside in the crisp night air right on time.

"Would you mind going to my house instead of a bar? That way I can let Nancy leave for the day and check on Cam too?"

"Fine." As they walked to their cars, breath frosting the air, Dev asked, "How's Patty?"

"Better. Badly broken right leg that required surgery, but she should make a full recovery."

"Good to hear."

They each climbed into their vehicles parked in the half-empty lot. Dev followed Val home. It was fine. It was just a simple talk. Nothing to be nervous about, he told himself, even as a small tremor of anticipation shimmered through him.

By the time they reached Val's house, Nancy was already waiting at the door and Dev felt like his skin was too tight for his body. Stepping into the quiet living room, nothing about this felt simple. It felt complicated and fraught with the previous night's kiss dangling tantalizingly between them like forbidden fruit. While Val went to check on Cam, Dev took off his coat then sent a quick text to his mother, letting her know where he was so she wouldn't worry.

She texted him back telling him to have fun.

Fun wasn't how Dev would describe the conversation they were about to have.

After the kiss, it felt like they were playing with fire and Dev didn't want to get burned again. And this was Val, a man who'd once been his closest friend and confidant. He couldn't relax, couldn't forget his decision to stay alone, stay safe. He was just so tired. Tired of being lonely. Tired of wanting things he couldn't have.

He closed his eyes and rested his head back against the sofa cushions, closing his eyes for a second, his mom's words reverberating in his exhausted brain.

Have fun.

If only it were that simple. Honestly, Dev couldn't remember the last time he'd done something just for fun, and not out of a sense of duty or responsibility or guilt. Even during his marriage, there'd always been something that had held him back from truly letting go. But something about seeing Val again seemed to have knocked his inner barriers loose, and now Dev felt far too exposed, all these dangerous emotions roiling inside him—desire, fear, need, hesitation. Because all of it was building up inside him like a powder keg.

And his undeniable chemistry with Val might just be the spark that would make him explode.

* * *

Val thanked Nancy and watched her leave, then went to check on Cam. His son was sound asleep, and as he closed Cam's bedroom door quietly and headed back toward the living room, his heart cartwheeled in his chest. It was just him and Dev now. The man he'd kissed last night. The man he hadn't stopped thinking about since they'd been reunited weeks ago. He ran a hand through his messy hair then called down the hall, "I'm going to hop in the shower quick and clean up. Make yourself at home and help yourself to anything you like. I'll be right out."

"Okay," Dev called back from the living room, his deep voice only making Val's adrenaline surge.

He hurried through a scrub down and shave, then changed into comfy sweats and socks before hurrying back out to make sure Dev hadn't suddenly decided to make a run for it while he'd been gone.

Nope. He was still there, sitting at the kitchen table with two plates, each with a sandwich on them, and a bag of potato chips between them. At Val's surprised look, Dev smiled. "What? You asked me to make food and since I'm not a cook like you, I took the easy route. PB and

J and chips. Not exactly a nutritional bonanza, but enough to fill us up for now."

Touched by the thoughtfulness, Val took a seat at the table. It had been a long time since someone had taken care of him like this. Usually, he was the caretaker, which was fine. He liked being needed, but having Dev care for him in this small way was nice too.

"Thanks," Val said, taking a sip from the glass of water Dev had set next to his plate. He really was starving, so dove into his food. Dev did too, and soon they were both happily eating away in companionable silence. It wasn't until they were both done and cleaning up that the old uncertainty reared its head again inside Val. He'd invited Dev here to talk about things. About that kiss specifically and what, if anything, they wanted to do about it. But now that the moment was upon them, he wasn't sure how to start. "Quite a day, huh?"

"Yep." Dev was rinsing their plates before putting them in the dishwasher. He was turned away from Val, allowing him time to admire the man's taut butt in those black pants he wore. Dev was built like a runner, which he was, or a racehorse—all sleek lines and lithe strength. Val swallowed hard, imagining those long, lanky limbs entwined with his amongst the sheets of his bed, breaths mingled, lost in passion and promise...

Oh, boy.

"So..." Dev finally shut the dishwasher and turned to face Val, who looked away quickly, face hot. "About that talk."

"Yeah." Val pulled two bottles of ale out of the fridge, handing one to Dev before leading him into the living room where they took a seat on the sofa. Val steeled himself for the necessary conversation ahead. He knew he wanted Dev, but he also knew that Dev was an emotional minefield right now too. Capable of blowing all the progress they'd made toward repairing their connection sky-high if Val made one wrong move at this point. So, he intended to let Dev take the lead here. Tell Val what he wanted and needed, and Val would do his best to fulfill that, whatever it was. As long as he continued to have Dev in his life, that's what mattered. He took a deep breath and twisted the cap off his ale, took a long swig, grateful for the cold liquid to soothe his burning throat as he said, "How do you feel about what happened?"

Dev's dark brows rose as he looked over at Val. "How do I feel about it?"

"Yes." Val nodded, feeling like the next few

minutes would affect everything going forward. "You kissed me. Why?"

"Jesus, Val." Dev took a long swallow of his own ale, his normally neat hair disheveled after what was probably hours of running his fingers through it anxiously, if Val had to guess. After the accident, and what had happened last night, Dev had to be turning it all over in his head. Even jittery and brooding, every cell in Val's body was vibrating like a tuning fork at Dev's closeness now, and he craved more of him, as much of him as he could get. He couldn't remember ever being so attuned to someone before, or wanting them as much as he did Dev. But he wouldn't touch him. Not yet. Not until he made it clear what he needed. Val had to be smart about this to avoid ruining everything. And not just between him and Dev, but there was Cam to consider too. Cam really liked Dev, and the boy had already lost someone he cared for. He didn't want his son to experience that again, if he could help it.

Dev frowned, fiddling with his glasses again as he cleared his throat, looking so flustered that Val wanted to hug him and tell him it would be okay, but didn't dare. "I don't know how I feel about it," he said finally. He took another long gulp of ale before cursing under his breath. "No. That's not true. I feel scared about it. Because I never wanted to need anyone like this again after what happened with Tom. And I certainly never expected it to be you, Val."

Val got that. All this had caught him by surprise too, but he knew it went deeper for Dev, with what he'd been through. "It shouldn't have happened. There are so many reasons why we should never do that again. You have Cam to worry about and a life here that I know nothing about. And I'm not sure I can ever open myself up to that again. We're so different Val. We always were."

"Is that what you want? To stop it now?" Val leaned forward. "It's your call, Dev. I don't want anyone to get hurt here, including Cam. That's why I wanted to talk about it now, before we did anything else." He glanced at the hallway then sat back again. "Tell me how you're feeling."

Dev shook his head, looking painfully confused. "That's the problem. I don't want to feel anything."

Val squeezed his eyes shut, knowing what it took for Dev to admit that after what he'd been through. "I get that. I think we've both experienced way more heartache than any person deserves in our lives. Especially the past couple of years."

"Exactly." Dev stood then, pacing the living room. "I don't trust emotions, don't trust myself either, after Tom. I never want to feel that raw and helpless again. I can't risk putting myself through that again."

Val understood where he was coming from, but that didn't lessen his disappointment that the possibility of more between them was over before it started. He should be happy about it. Keeping things strictly in the friend zone between them made life a lot easier. No worries about Cam losing his new friend Dev. No risk that Val wouldn't be able to stop his own emotions from crossing the line from casual to complicated, which would be so easy for him where Dev was concerned. It was good. It was fine. He shrugged and forced a half-hearted smile because it didn't feel good at all. "So that's it then."

Dev stopped near a window across from Val, and stared out through the blinds and the night sky beyond, his back to Val. "Today, at the accident scene, when I first got there and I heard your voice calling for help, I panicked. All I could think about was what if you were in one of those cars, hurt, trapped? What if it was Cam in there?" He huffed out a breath, his shoulders sagging. "I'm not sure what I'd do without you.

And it terrified me, Val. Because I don't want to need anyone like that again. Not after what my dad did. Not after what Tom did."

Val set his ale bottle beside Dev's on the coffee table, then got up and walked over to stand beside him, wanting to be near him, lend support, but still not quite touching. "I get it. I thought about Cam too. About you. What I'd do if I was one of those poor victims. What I'd regret in my life if it was suddenly over."

"And what would you regret?" Dev asked quietly, still staring straight ahead out the window.

For a quick second, Val thought about lying, but tonight was all about being honest, and Dev deserved the truth after enduring so many lies in his past. "You. I'd regret not being with you, in any way I could."

The embrace was so fast that even looking back later, Val still wasn't sure how it had happened, but next thing he knew, he was in Dev's arms, his face buried in the side of Dev's neck, inhaling his good Dev scent—soap and fabric softener and a hint of spice. Dev held him tight, like he'd never let him go, like he needed Val so desperately, and Val just held on, needing to be needed, needing to fix whatever was wrong inside him, to protect this connection from harm.

Eventually, Dev said into the hair near Val's temple, "I shouldn't do this."

"What? Need comfort?" Val said against his skin, resisting the urge to nuzzle him.

Dev pulled back then, his dark gaze hot behind his glasses. "It's not just comfort, Val. Never has been for us. Not now."

The words hung there, glowing like a beacon between them. Or a warning of danger ahead.

Either way, they both stood there, in each other's arms, gazes locked, frozen, as if caught between a bad decision and a worse need. Finally, Dev squeezed his eyes shut and whispered, the words ragged and so quiet Val had to lean in closer just to hear them, "If we do this, it can't mean anything more than sex, Val. That's all I can give you."

Val took that in, nose to nose with him, blood pounding through his body, every fiber of his being screaming for more, for release, for Dev. If no strings, no emotions, were the rules Dev needed to make this happen, Val would agree, because he wanted Dev. Period. More than his next breath. So, he'd do it, keep his heart out of it. Val wasn't sure how exactly, but he'd figure it out. Because staring up into Dev's huge, dark eyes, seeing his lips wet and parted and so close Val could almost taste them, all that strength and warmth and hardness right there against him, he would've promised just about anything to have more of it, more of him. "I'll take it."

Then they were kissing again, Dev's hands clenched in Val's hair, pulling him in tighter as his lips devoured Val's. By the time they pulled away again slightly, they were both breathless.

"What next?" Val growled, leaning in for a second round, only to be stopped by Dev tightening his fingers in his hair, stopping him. Val was a switch in bed, taking either role depending on who he was with—sometimes dominant, sometimes submissive as the mood suited. And Dev needed the power here too. He was fine with it—in fact, it turned him on even more. Val would happily be Dev's fantasy all night long if Dev was there with him. His slow, wicked smile grew. "Tell me what you need."

Dev cursed again, a muscle ticking near his tight jaw, his hot gaze searing Val from the inside out. "You. I need you."

"Then have me," Val teased, relishing the pull on his scalp that earned him.

"And you're good with casual," Dev growled. "Nothing more here than sex?"

In answer, Val ground against him, letting him feel just how all right he was with it. "I am."

"Good." Dev picked him up then, carrying Val down the hall, saying against his lips, "Which room?"

"Last one on the left," Val murmured into his mouth, not wanting to break contact for a second. He kissed along Dev's jaw, knocking his glasses askew, but it didn't matter. Nothing mattered except the fact they were inside Val's bedroom now. Dev shut the door and locked it. Val took off Dev's glasses and set them on the dresser for safekeeping, turning back around to find Dev watching him in the moon-shadowed darkness.

This time their kiss went deeper, flared brighter. They shed their clothes, then moved together onto the bed, each moan and groan caught and swallowed in each other's mouths to avoid detection. Sweet torture, especially as Dev's hands moved lower, with careful intention, exploring the landscape of Val's body as if memorizing it for the first time. And as much as he didn't want to rush, to take this first time slow, it had been far too long for Val, and he doubted he could last.

For so long, Dev had been an untouchable dream, so self-sufficient and contained. An enigma. But tonight, Val saw beneath the facade. With each stroke and caress, every lick and nip, Dev allowed Val closer, deeper, until there was nothing left between them but the truth of their desire. He wished it could go on forever. He was afraid it would disappear too soon.

Then Val surrendered to Dev, to sensation, exploring, tasting, teasing, moving together as the pressure built until they both went over the brink, finally collapsing on the bed, spent and sated.

Afterward, Val lay cocooned in Dev, limbs tangled in the quiet night, filled with the blessed satisfaction of finally getting exactly what he'd needed. Finally, he found the strength to move slightly and whisper in Dev's ear, savoring his slight shiver when Val's lips grazed the sensitive skin there. "All right?"

"Yes," Dev whispered back, voice gruff, smiling against Val's cheek. "Can't remember the last time I've been this relaxed."

"Same." Val grinned, feeling inordinately proud of himself for giving Dev that gift as they both gave in to sleep. For now, anyway, everything felt right with his world. And if complications arrived later, well, he'd worry about those then.

CHAPTER SEVEN

DEV FUMBLED WITH the bright blue Frisbee before tossing it into the open sky.

It had been a little over three weeks now since their first night together. They were into November now and…well, he was still trying to figure it all out. They'd both agreed to keep things friendly regardless, especially for Cam, who'd grown even more fond of Dev it seemed. And so far, so good.

They were spending a lovely fall Sunday in a field in Minnehaha Park, playing sports, though in general that was not his strong suit. He'd always been the kid who was happier figuring out the season stats for teams while Val was the star player. Still, they'd meshed well together.

Both in and out of bed…

Distracted now by the thought of them in bed together the night before, Val beneath him, around him, calling out Dev's name as he climaxed, he threw the Frisbee way too wide. Val leaped for it anyway, missing and tumbling to the ground. He got right back up again, running to get the errant Frisbee from where it had landed near a tree, Cam sprinting after him—taking after Val in his athletic abilities, apparently. Dev watched them from a safe distance, glad to be out of the fray.

"Show-offs," he called, as Val and Cam ran toward him, grinning. He enjoyed spending time with them both, and they were settling into a nice, comfortable ease. Not that he was letting himself get too used to it. They'd agreed to keep it all casual, no strings attached, which meant no emotions, no binding attachments. So far, so good. And the sex…well, that was amazing. Val seemed to sense what he needed before Dev could even ask for it, their yin and yang opposition translating well there too.

Sometimes, Dev worried that Val was giving more to make things work than he was, but he never complained and seemed happy just to have more time with Dev. And Dev was happy to have their friendship back too, and a new bond with Cam, so it worked out well for him. Cam reminded Dev so much of himself at that age in so many areas—the boy's interest in science and space, his love of building models—

though Cam was much more outgoing than Dev ever was or would be.

And if, occasionally, Dev's old doubts and fears surfaced because things seemed to have fallen into place so easily, maybe too easily, well, he just needed time to adjust, he told himself. That was all. Easy wasn't something he trusted, among other things.

"I thought you might break something going after that Frisbee," Dev said to Val as he and Cam reached him on the field.

"Hey, I'm thirty-six, not three hundred and six," Val teased back as he stopped a few feet in front of Dev, his blue eyes sparkling with mirth as he handed the Frisbee to Cam. "Ready to eat now, buddy? I'm starving!"

"Yes!" Cam yelled, racing for the blanket they'd spread out on the ground under an ancient oak tree. Bright yellow and orange and red leaves scattered the ground, and the whole scene felt cozy and comfortable and—even Dev had to admit—pretty damn perfect.

You convinced yourself things were perfect with Tom too...

Dev shoved that unwanted doubt aside as they all settled on the blanket and began unpacking the basket of food Dev had ordered from his favorite local deli. He checked the label then passed Val a sandwich wrapped neatly in parchment paper. "Turkey and Swiss with all the trimmings, your favorite."

"You remembered?" Val asked as he took it, looking a bit astonished.

"How could I forget?" Dev snorted. "You ate those things every chance you got back in med school." He forced his gaze away from Val's now-beaming face, his chest squeezing with affection and something more he didn't want to think about too much right then. *Feeling more* wasn't allowed here, per his own rules.

Next, he pulled out a PB and J for Cam. "Crunchy with homemade strawberry preserves."

"Yum! Thanks, Dr. Dev!" Cam beamed too as he grabbed his food, and this time Dev couldn't help grinning right back, giving himself more emotional latitude there. He was used to relating to his young patients, forming a bond with them to allow for the most effective treatments. He'd trained for this, used his skills for this, so it felt safer to him. That's how he rationalized it to himself anyway.

"Oh, my God, this is so good," Val said around a hearty bite of his sandwich, giving a deep groan of pleasure that should have been illegal in all fifty states because of the effect it had on Dev's body. Then Val gave him a covert wink. "You're amazing."

Dev averted his gaze, hiding his heated face by digging out his own food—chicken salad on whole wheat bread with all the trimmings. The first delicious bite was just as good as he remembered from his med school days. As they ate, he avoided making eye contact with Val by watching a pair of squirrels chase each other across the field.

Cam finished first, as usual. For such a small kid, he could pack away food like no one's business. He scrambled to his feet to throw away his trash in a nearby can, then bounded back to the blanket with the relentless energy of childhood. "Can we play basketball now, Dr. Dev?" He pointed to the empty court a short distance away. "Please?"

Glad to have something to do besides sit there and lust after Val, Dev devoured the last bite of his sandwich then climbed to his feet to throw away his own trash. "Sure. But I have to warn you, I'm not very good."

They shot some hoops for a while, or at least Cam did. Dev basically ran after the ball when he missed. After that, he and Val pushed Cam on the swings, higher and higher, until the boy's laughter filled the air like music. Dev couldn't help noticing Val's muscles ripple as he guided the swing. The man was beautiful, no other way to describe it. His heart squeezed a little harder.

Mine.

Oh, no. No, no, no. Dev froze at the sudden rush of forbidden possessiveness that filled him as panic sank its teeth in around his edges. They were friends. Good friends. Friends with benefits. That was what he'd wanted, what Val had agreed to. He didn't want more than that, wasn't ready for more.

Am I?

He stumbled back a step and caught himself with a hand on the swing set. Val gave him a curious glance, but thankfully didn't mention anything about Dev's odd behavior.

Dev wasn't ready for another relationship. Not with Val, not with anyone. And yes, they'd agreed to a no-strings-attached fling, but he also didn't want to ruin his second chance at a great friendship with Val. He wasn't in love with the one person who knew him better than anyone—the good, the bad and the downright ugly—and supported him anyway. Val was light and optimistic and a steady shoulder to cry on. What he and Val had now was…indispensable to him.

He refused to screw that up by getting emotions involved.

Then there was Cam. He'd grown close to the boy too, treating him like the son he'd never had. He wouldn't risk the bond they'd developed by screwing up things with Val by doing something stupid, like getting his heart involved then having to walk away when it all fell apart, because love always fell apart. Usually at the worst possible time. No. This was all sex, no emotion. Exactly what he was looking for. He took a deep breath and steeled his resolve to maintain their agreement, remain friends, remain constant in each other's lives from here on out and not get the L-word involved at all.

They could share their bodies without their hearts messing it all up.

Easy-peasy. For a logical guy like himself, he should be able to detach at the drop of a hat.

No fuss. No muss.

"Higher, Uncle Val! Dr. Dev, look!" Cam shouted, kicking his legs out to touch the puffy white clouds above.

"Be careful," Dev called back, trying for a playful tone. But the sudden gruffness in his voice made the words sound more like a dire warning. Mainly for himself.

Keep it light. Keep it fun. Keep things easy.

It was getting late now, and streaks of orange and pink began to creep over the horizon as sunset grew closer. It came earlier and earlier this time of year. Another warning that time was fleeting. *Don't screw this up.*

Flustered and frowning, Dev checked his smartwatch. "We should head back home soon."

"Sure," Val said, glancing at Dev curiously as he scooped Cam off the swing and into his arms. "Everything okay?"

Dev nodded, not trusting his words at that point.

On the way home to Val's, they stopped to pick up a few essentials at a local grocery store, the fluorescent glow of the overhead lights a stark contrast to the gathering twilight outside. The trio navigated the aisles together, Val grabbing milk and bread while Cam directed from his seat in their Racecart—a shopping cart made to look like a racecar with the basket in the front—pointing out his favorite snacks with the glee of a tiny emperor.

For some reason, shopping together felt strangely intimate and domestic, but Dev was grateful for the distraction as he continued to process what had happened back at the park. His panic had subsided at least, allowing him to think more clearly about the situation. It wasn't like he didn't care for Val at all. He did. They'd known each other a long time. Of course he cared for him. For Cam too, since the two of them were now a package deal. Perhaps that's where the surge of protectiveness had come from, he reasoned. Yes. That sounded totally natural and normal. No need to go overboard and push things to the next forbidden level. It wasn't love. Nope. It was kinship, deep and abiding. That was all.

Satisfied now that he'd found a plausible explanation for his irrational deviation from their plan, Dev turned his focus back to the new things Val had added to their cart. Potatoes, bacon and a package of steaks for the grill. An old memory from their med school days rose, making Dev chuckle. "Remember when you nearly set your apartment on fire trying to make filet mignon in the oven?"

"Hey, I was following a recipe from the Food Network. I couldn't help it if the butter browned quicker than I expected." Val shook his head, his laugh reverberating deep inside Dev. "And there was never an actual fire. Just lots of smoke that set off the alarm." He shrugged and added a bottle of spices. "That's why I grill them now."

"Can I get some of this, Uncle Val?" Cam

asked, pointing at a box with a neon green monster on the front. "Please?"

"You have cereal at home, buddy." Val reached forward to ruffle Cam's hair. "Maybe next week."

As they approached an open checkout lane, the cashier smiled. "What a lovely family."

Dev and Val froze midway through emptying the cart as Cam answered. "Oh, we're not a family. Not yet anyway. Right, Uncle Val?"

Val recovered first, placing the rest of the stuff on the counter while Dev escaped to the far end of the lane to bag up their purchases. Cam continued to chat to the cashier, completely oblivious to the fact he'd just blown all Dev's perfectly rational explanations clean out of the water, because for just a second, he'd wished it was true. That they were a real family.

Oh, boy.

This was bad. So, so bad.

Dev swallowed so hard it clicked. Cam's answer had been completely honest. They'd both been careful not to give him any impression that they were together as a couple. To Cam, he and Val were just good friends, which was why Dev had spent more time at their house over the last few weeks. They'd thought they were handling it well. That no one would get hurt here when it ended. But Cam adding on those last three words—*not yet anyway*—made it clear that he hoped for more. Which was a problem, because whatever this was between him and Val would eventually end. Things like this always did. And when Dev was gone, Cam would be hurt and that was the last thing Dev wanted.

As he shoved items into the cloth bags they'd brought in with them, he continued to berate himself for not sticking to the plan, for thinking somehow that this arrangement would work out in everyone's favor just because they'd made some stupid agreement. He obviously wasn't ready for this. Maybe he never would be, given how his marriage turned out. And yet, he'd gone ahead with Val, knowing it was a risk. Knowing it could all go sideways again. Knowing it could go too far.

Driving home passed in a blur of self-recriminations, and next thing Dev knew, they were carrying the groceries inside Val's house.

The soft hum of the refrigerator cycling on echoed through the silence as Val put away the groceries and Cam went to his room to get ready for bed. They were all still so stuffed from lunch that no one had wanted dinner. Dev had no appetite anyway, too full of stress for much else—or at least he thought so, until Cam raced back into the kitchen a few minutes later to let Val know he was ready for his bedtime story. Instead of going back to his bedroom though, the boy ran over to Dev and hugged his legs. "Goodnight, Dr. Dev. I love you!"

Dev gripped the edge of the counter and reminded himself to breathe, throat tight and heart thundering. Yep. Things had definitely gone too far, and it was up to him to put on the brakes before it was too late.

After tucking Cam in for the night, Val joined Dev in the living room. He could feel the tension radiating off Dev from the other end of the couch, and saw the slight sheen of sweat on his forehead. Yep. He was flipping out, probably because of Cam's sudden proclamation of love earlier. Honestly, Val had been a little shocked by it too, but knew emotions of any kind were touchy, scary subjects for Dev, so he tried to hide that as much as possible. They'd agreed to keep things light, easy, and make sure Cam wasn't hurt by any of it. So his son dropping the L-word was a bombshell, to say the least. And while he fully supported Cam in feeling his feels, Val was also trying to teach him that not every emotion needed to be expressed as you were having it.

Sometimes it was better to wait for the perfect time and place.

Or never, in Val's case, considering the agreement they'd made.

So, even if he did want to do what Cam had done—wrap his arms around Dev and tell him he loved him—he wouldn't. Especially right now, with that haunted, shell-shocked look on Dev's face. Instead, Val sat cautiously and tried to think of a way to avoid the gravity threatening to pull them both under by downplaying the importance of Cam's statement. "You know, he told his teacher last week that he loved her too."

It was true. Cam was still the happiest kid Val had ever met, despite what he'd been through. And that joy had just grown since Dev had spent more time at their house. For Val too, and the last thing he wanted was to ruin the wonderful thing they had going and scare Dev away by confessing feelings he wasn't supposed to have. He'd known the rules going into this, and had promised to keep his heart out of the mix. At the time, he'd honestly thought he could, but he just wasn't built that way.

Neither was Cam. Must be genetic, getting attached to people so deeply.

Dev finally turned toward Val, frowning, as

if he'd just realized Val was there, "Cam told his teacher he loved her?"

"Yeah." Val sighed and stretched his legs out in front of him, trying to look relaxed, even though he wasn't. "The kids at school teased him for a week afterward too."

Dev didn't respond. If anything, he looked even more unhappy, which put Val more on edge.

This was all spinning out of control too fast. He wished they could go back to that afternoon in the park, when things had been fun and light and full of sweet connection. After Vicki had died, he'd felt like a piece of him had been buried with her. A piece he'd feared would never feel happiness again. Then Dev had returned to town and his joy had returned tenfold, only he was supposed to keep that secret because it wasn't allowed. Val squeezed his eyes shut and inhaled deeply. God, why did he have to make things so complicated? Why did he have to fall in love with Dev when he shouldn't?

Because I'm an idiot.

Dev stood and raked his hands through his hair. "This is exactly what I feared would happen."

Val opened his eyes, preparing himself for battle. He wasn't ready to lose Dev yet, and he'd fight to keep this thing going between them for as long as he could, even if it meant denying his own heart. "He's seven, Dev. He'll be fine. I'll talk to him." He leaned forward, resting his forearms on his knees, his hands dangling between them. "Don't freak out, okay? He's good. We're all good."

"Are we?" Dev shook his head, throwing his hands up, his tone exasperated. "Because I don't feel good, Val. Not about any of this…" He huffed out a frustrated breath. "I don't know what we're doing here anymore."

Val knew he was on fragile ground here, and rather than chance a full meltdown of things, he tried to lower the temperature of the situation by avoiding the subject entirely. He grabbed the remote and clicked on the TV, scrolling through the on-screen guide to find something good to watch, and patted the seat beside him. "How about you sit down and we decompress a bit, watch a show?" He glanced up and met Dev's gaze. "This doesn't have to be any more than we let it be."

Dev's dark eyes held Val's for a few more tense seconds before he finally settled back on the sofa and stared at the TV screen, where a weekly medical drama that was so far from real life that it was laughable played out. Val hoped maybe the soap opera of the love lives of the characters might help divert attention away from their own mess, allowing some of the tension in the air to dissipate.

It didn't seem to work though, because next thing he knew, Dev was on his feet again. "I should go."

"Go?" Val followed him to the foyer. "I thought you were staying tonight."

Dev tugged on his coat before facing Val again. "I think it's best if we all get a little space right now." Val opened his mouth to argue, but Dev held up a hand, cutting him off. "I know you said Cam telling people he loves them is normal, but I said from the start of this I don't want him hurt when this is over because he's too attached to me. I know too well what it's like to be abandoned by someone you love."

Heart aching, Val stepped closer and slid his arms inside Dev's coat, his hands at Dev's waist. "I don't want my son hurt either. But I also don't want to lose what we have. Please stay."

Dev grabbed Val's wrists, his heat encompassing them as he whispered, "I can't."

"Sure you can." Val broke free of his grasp and ran his palms up Dev's sweater-covered chest to twine them behind his neck, toying with the hair at his nape. "Just take off your coat and we'll go to bed."

"Val," Dev said, his voice lowering to a growl as Val leaned in to nuzzle his neck.

"It will be fine. I promise." Val leaned back to look Dev in the eye. "Trust me."

A muscle ticked near Dev's tense jaw and Val flicked his tongue over it, causing Dev to fist the back of Val's shirt, pulling him even closer, if that were possible. "You know I can't."

"Yes, you can," Val said, before pulling him into a heated kiss that soon turned into a wildfire.

They somehow managed to make the trip to Val's bedroom blindly amidst a flurry of kisses and swallowed groans. Dev's coat ended up on the floor as soon as the bedroom door was locked behind them, cocooning them in shadowed intimacy. Val tugged Dev's sweater off over his head, then removed his own shirt, leaving them both naked from the waist up. He couldn't seem to be able to stop touching Dev, stroking him. "God, I swear you're like a drug to me. I can't get enough of you."

Dev flattened Val against the wall, skin to skin, grinding against him while he kissed and nipped the side of Val's neck. "I need you so badly."

"Yes," Val gasped, holding him closer, tracing his fingers lower over the planes of Dev's taut stomach, then around to cup his tight butt through his jeans, savoring every contour, the hidden strength, the solidity of him being there, right where he belonged. "I'm here. Whatever you want. I'll always be here for you, Dev. Promise."

"Stop it. Stop saying that. It isn't true. We're not doing that." Dev ground his hard length against Val's until they both moaned low into each other's mouths. "We agreed. Just sex. That's it."

At that moment, Val wanted him so badly, he would've agreed with anything Dev said just to keep him there, touching him like that. "Whatever you need."

"No." Dev pulled back, his expression angry, their jagged breaths mingling, the air charged. "Tell me what this is. Say it, so I know we're both on the same page."

Mind swirling with adrenaline and desire, Val panted, "Just sex. Just for fun."

Then they were kissing, their mutual need igniting into a wildfire fueled by past regrets and present desires. Dev slid his fingers slid through Val's hair, banishing any lingering space between them. When they finally parted, they each stripped away their remaining clothes then stretched out on the bed, bodies entwined, hearts beating in sync. Val took both their hard lengths in hand, stroking, caressing, driving them both nearer to the edge of oblivion. Dev thrust against him, harder, faster, seeking his release, his mouth hot on Val's ear. And when pleasure overtook them both, they held each other close, all the fears and uncertainties vanishing beneath a rush of endorphins.

As they lay together in the afterglow, exhaustion threatened to pull Val under into slumber, but he fought against it, snuggling into Dev's side, knowing what he'd promised. Knowing he'd already broken their agreement by falling so far and so deep for Dev that he'd never find his way out. This had gone beyond sex for him after their first night together, but he'd denied it. To Dev and to himself because he didn't want to lose Dev again. He didn't want to lie to Dev, but telling him the truth at that point might drive him away forever.

CHAPTER EIGHT

DEV WOKE UP PREDAWN the next morning and carefully got out of bed to avoid waking Val, who was still snoozing away beside him. The room was cast in shadows, except for a small Lego figurine on the nightstand highlighted by a shaft of light from a streetlight outside. He picked it up and brushed his thumb against the tiny plastic contours, each bump a reminder of Cam's earnest proclamation the night before.

Goodnight, Dr. Dev. I love you...

Chest constricted, Dev put the figurine back fast, as if it had burned him. God, what the hell was wrong with him? He never should have started this thing with Val in the first place. It made him want things that weren't possible, things he didn't think he was capable of giving, like his heart. Why did he think he could handle this?

What a mess.

With a sigh, he stood to collect his clothes off

the bedroom floor, his mind churning through images from the day before, stopping repeatedly on images of Val and Cam together. He'd walked into their lives knowing he wasn't what they needed, but it had been too tempting to resist. And Cam was the one who'd be hurt the most if he stayed, if he kept pretending. It was bad enough he cared so much now.

And, regardless of what Val had said about Cam's teacher, those words weren't meaningless to Dev. He took another deep breath, lungs aching, like there wasn't enough oxygen in the room, in the world, for him. He needed to get out of here, figure all this out, decide how to handle this thing between them going forward.

He tugged on his jeans and shirt, feeling broken and bitter, berating himself for his own foolishness.

Val deserved better. Cam deserved better.

And since Dev had started this whole disaster, it was his responsibility to fix it now. By giving them all a chance to cool down and get some distance from things, to look at the situation logically.

He snorted softly as he searched for his missing sock. Logically? While Val was the epitome of calm rationality in the ER, outside of work his strong suit was his emotions, which only terrified Dev more.

Because Val knew him so well, and if he sensed that Dev might have crossed the line of their agreement, and let his own emotions get involved, then…

No. Distance was the best answer now.

A break. They all had busy schedules. They probably wouldn't even notice he was gone. They'd be fine without Dev. And it wasn't forever, just until things were back under control again.

He shoved his feet into his sneakers then picked up his coat, walking to the window again to peer through the curtains at the approaching sunrise, the dark night giving way to brilliant purples and oranges and pinks. It felt like an omen, a sign that Dev was making the right choice here for all of them. To avoid the risk of getting hurt even more. Dev didn't think he could bear that. He cared more for Val and Cam then he had for anyone in a long, long time—including Tom—but it was best to go for now, before Cam got even more attached to him. Let them all adjust to Dev not being around. They'd been good before him. They'd be good after him too.

But his heart ached like someone had gouged

it out with a dull spoon. Part of him wanted nothing more than to crawl back into bed with Val and hold onto him for dear life. Which was exactly why he had to leave. He needed to re-build his walls, to protect everyone, himself included.

"Hey…" A groggy Val rolled over then, sheets rustling, looking rumpled and ridiculously handsome, squinting at Dev. "It's still early. Come back to bed for a little longer."

Every cell in his body yearned to do just that, to climb back into Val's arms, sink into the imaginary comfort of the fantasy they'd built. But he had to stay firm, so he forced himself to shake his head. "Sorry. I can't. Need to go. Early shift this morning." Thankfully, his voice sounded steadier than his resolve. "Go back to sleep."

Val's sleepy blue gaze narrowed. "What's wrong?"

"Nothing's wrong." Dev backed toward the door, hating that he was lying to Val but not able to tell him the truth either. God, he'd let him-self become such a hypocrite. Another strike against him. He wanted to go slink under a rock somewhere and hide. "I'm just thinking about my schedule and all the prep I have to do ahead of time."

He could just tell Val that his feelings had changed, that he was scared and shaken and unsure what to do now—but that was a conversation he wasn't prepared to have that early in the morning, so best to leave it for later. Right now, he just had to get the hell out of there before Val picked up on anything else in his behavior.

But Val let it go for once, flopping back onto the mattress and yawning. "Fine. Lunch later?"

"Uh, I don't know." Dev had his hand on the bedroom door handle now, the metal cool beneath his palm, eager for escape. "Text me later and we'll figure it out."

Or not.

He fled then, like a coward, grabbing his coat and rushing out of the house and into his car, driving back to his mother's house to shower and change for work. By the time he made it to the medical center, it was nearly time for his shift to start. He felt tired and achy and like he'd been run over by a train. Repeatedly. He slumped to his office and booted up his computer, then sat down at his desk to go over his case files for the day, hoping a cup of coffee would help. And he'd been right about one thing at least. His schedule was nuts for that day and for the foreseeable future.

Work had always been a balm for him though,

so he was grateful for it now. Clicking through his patient files, he made notes and lost himself in the details, the heat blasting from the vent overhead the only sound filling the otherwise silent office. Matt Warden and his mother were due in for another follow-up today, sans Val this time, and from the latest blood work results, the teen was continuing to improve. Some good news at last.

The rest of that morning rushed by. The afternoon too. And despite what he'd said earlier that day, no text ever came through from Val, which was a relief. In fact, Dev had almost thought he'd dodged a bullet there, until Val arrived in person, just after practice hours. The rest of the staff had gone for the day, so it was just Dev there in his office.

"Hey," he said from the doorway. "Sorry I forgot to text. Time got away from me. Have time for a break now?"

"Actually, no." Dev hedged, his heart tripping just at the sight of Val. Knowing he was in big trouble here, he focused on rifling through his drawers to find the notepad he was missing. "I'm buried under documentation that has to be done before I leave tonight. Maybe another time?"

"How about dinner later then?" Val straightened, looking bummed. "I'm making spaghetti. Vicki's recipe. Your favorite. I'll save you some and you can heat it up when you get there."

Dev found the notepad, throat tight. He reminded himself of his decision to give them all space, and showing up at Val's house again tonight went against that entirely. Deep down, he knew the separation was for everyone's good, even though it felt like the exact opposite. "Sorry, but I can't. Late meeting, then I promised my mom I'd help with some projects around the house."

Val frowned as he walked into the office and leaned on the edge of Dev's desk. "Are you sure there's nothing wrong?"

"Positive." Dev avoided his gaze by staring intently at his laptop screen. He really didn't want to do this right now. "See you later."

"Yeah. I hope so," Val said, straightening and backing toward to the door. "You're sure you're okay?"

"Yep," Dev managed to squeak out. "I'm great."

"See you later then."

He waited until he heard the elevator ding and the doors close again, before he slumped in his chair and covered his face. He was already second-guessing his decision, which didn't make it any easier, but he was determined to see it through, to protect them all the only way he knew how—by making himself scarce.

Soon, one day turned into a week, then two, and the less Dev spoke to or saw Val and Cam, the more he expected his craving to see them would ease, but it didn't. Because each time he went down to the ER for a consult, he found himself peeking around every corner, hoping to see Val. Not that he was ready to have that talk with him yet, about the status of things between them. Several times he'd picked up his phone, intending to just get it over and done with, but at the last second, he'd lose his courage and find another excuse to put it off for just one more day, and somehow, he'd almost convinced himself they could continue like this indefinitely.

But, of course, they couldn't. Deep down he knew that. And so, when he finally ran into Val late one night at the hospital, after a long, grueling shift during which Dev had lost two patients despite his best efforts, it almost felt like fate. It happened outside the staff break room on the first floor. Val's weary expression spoke of frustration and sleepless nights and Dev's first thought was to turn around and go back the way he'd come. But he couldn't, because Val had already seen him, and besides, Dev was too exhausted to avoid this anymore. The time had come to have it out, once and for all.

"Dev." The uncharacteristic harshness in Val's tone said he was clearly done with this nonsense. "Why are you avoiding us?"

Us. Not *me.* Because Cam was part of this too. Dev hid his wince as his stomach plunged to his toes, but he was too far into this mess to back out now. "I'm not avoiding you. I told you my schedule's crazy."

"Mine too, but I still find time for important things." Val followed him into the empty break room and shut the door behind them, the vending machines humming as they faced off. "Look, it's one thing if you don't want to sleep with me anymore. I'm an adult. I can take it. But Cam is just a kid. He cares about you. He thought you were his friend, and then you just disappeared on him like he didn't matter to you at all. I thought you of all people would know what that's like."

Ouch. A direct hit there to the soft underbelly of my decisions.

Time to explain himself, to make Val understand that this was what was best for all of them.

Even if it didn't feel like it now.

"I do know what it's like to be so attached

to someone or something, only to have it taken away. That's why I needed to slow things down, to give us all some space to cool off and think rationally about all this, so no one gets hurts. Especially Cam."

"He's seven, Dev," Val said, giving him a flat stare. "He can't even spell *rationally*, let alone understand it. How could you just dump him like that? I thought we had an agreement."

"We did," Dev said, scowling. "And I didn't dump him. I was going to see him again at some point, once I had things back under control." Defensiveness prickled inside him, making him feel like a naughty schoolboy getting scolded by the headmaster. He didn't like it one bit. He was trying to do them all a favor here. Why couldn't Val understand that? "Trust me. It's for the best."

Val's derisive snort had Dev's hackles rising. "Trust you? That's rich. Why should I, when you don't give me the same courtesy? I'm sick of this, Dev. Of feeling like I have to walk on eggshells around you so you don't get upset or spooked or whatever and take off again." He turned away, his tanned cheeks red and his blue eyes flashing with anger. "And you still left. I did everything you asked of me and you still walked away like we meant nothing to you."

"That's not…" Dev ground his teeth, stopping himself because he couldn't find the right words to say what he meant, because he was afraid anything he said would only push them farther apart. He'd already botched this conversation so far and only wanted to get out now before he caused more harm. "Look. You're right." He huffed out a breath and shook his head. "It's not you. It's me. I can't do this. I thought I could, but I can't. You did everything I asked, but I'm just not ready yet. Even for a meaningless fling."

Even as those last words emerged, Dev regretted them. Because they weren't even close to true.

He was leaving because he cared too much and it scared the hell out of him. Because somehow, regardless of all his efforts, what he and Val had shared over the past few weeks had become the most meaningful relationship of his life, and if it blew up in his face or was ripped away or crumbled before his eyes, like love usually did for him, he wasn't sure he could survive it.

"Meaningless fling?" Val blanched, his usual warm laugh icy cold now. "Right. Sure. Okay. My bad. We agreed to that, I suppose. But Cam didn't. You swore you wouldn't hurt him, Dev."

He stepped closer, furious hurt pulsing off him in waves. "Did you know he still asks about you every day? Asks when you're coming over again, or if we can go see Elaine." A muscle ticked near Val's hard jaw. "After everything he's been through, the last thing my son needs is someone else leaving him and that's exactly what you did. I don't care if you break my heart, but how dare you hurt my son? I don't want you near him ever again."

I don't care if you break my heart...

Confirmation of his deepest concerns—that they'd already grown more attached to each other than he'd wanted—only made Dev feel worse as guilt and regret twisted deeper in his gut, nearly dropping him to his knees. He'd only wanted to protect them all, so he'd done what he'd thought was best, but in the end, he hadn't protected anyone at all. He'd only made the pain worse. And now it was too late. "I didn't mean for any of this to happen, I swear. I thought it would be better this way. I thought Cam would forget about me and move on. You said yourself he needed to learn boundaries."

"Not this way!" Val's voice grew sharper and louder. "Jesus, Dev. And FYI, this is about as far from healthy boundaries as you can get. Healthy boundaries would be getting to know someone before giving them your heart. Healthy boundaries would be talking about things, not just running away and avoiding the situation. Those are the kinds of boundaries I want my son to learn. Not to be an emotionless, careless bastard who's scared to feel anything for fear it will break him."

Val stalked across the room then, scrubbing his hands over his face, while Dev stood rooted to the spot, unable to move, because Val was right. That was who'd he'd become. A walking, talking self-fulfilling prophecy. He'd expected this whole situation to fall apart at some point and boom, it had happened. He'd known better and he'd done it anyway. Val glanced at him then, the hurt in his eyes slicing into Dev's soul deeper than any scalpel. One long beat stretched into two, then three, until Dev finally found his voice again. "You're right. You and Cam deserved better. You always did. This is all my fault and you're both better off without me. I'm sorry. For everything."

Shame scalding him from the inside out, Dev walked out then, the white walls seeming to close in on him as his clamoring pulse drowned out every other noise. It was done. Over. He was safe and secure again. Alone. Just like he'd wanted. Even if it felt like Dev's heart would never recover.

He didn't need a heart.

Hearts only hurt you when they broke.

You're right. You and Cam deserved better. You always did...

As Val finished up his paperwork before leaving the ER for the night, Dev's words were running through his head on an endless loop. He liked being right as much as the next person, but this time it only made him feel worse. Because Dev wasn't the only one to blame here. After all, he'd crossed the line from fling to wanting forever a long time ago in their relationship—even though he'd sworn not to—and now he was so far gone he'd need a map to find his way back to normal. And for the first time in his life, Val had hidden his feelings away just to have more time with the man he loved. He'd betrayed them both by lying about it and it felt awful.

His whole life, people had told Val he cared too much, too soon, and eventually it would get him into trouble. In for a penny, in for a pound, as Vicki used to say. He'd never listened, never heeded the warnings, but he should have. Especially because there was more to worry about now than just himself. There was Cam too. God, he felt like the worst parent ever. How could he have been so stupid, so reckless? How did you explain to a kid that an adult he cared about didn't want to see him anymore because he was too damaged by the past? All those books he read to Cam every night covered a lot of emotional territory, but Val couldn't remember one that addressed this topic.

As he finished his last chart and headed for the staff locker room to get his coat, the lights of the hospital corridor blurred past him, his heavy steps carrying the weight of his bad decisions and his regrets.

How could he have thought going into this thing with Dev would be a win-win situation? It was so obvious now that it would never have worked, not when Dev had always had one foot out the door from the start, and Val had used their agreement as an excuse to hide the fact that he'd fallen hard and fast for his former best friend. Which made him just as much of a liar as Tom had been.

He drove home, parked in his driveway and cut the engine, resting his forehead against the steering wheel.

What the hell is wrong with me?

To Val, love was not something scary or

something to be hidden away, but in Dev's experience, it only brought hurt and humiliation. And regardless of his motives for not telling Dev how he really felt, Val felt as much at fault for how things had ended up between them as Dev.

With a sigh, he got out of the SUV and walked up to the front door. He should have stayed true to himself and led with his heart first, even if it would have ended their affair before it had started. At least then, he wouldn't have betrayed Dev and himself by lying. All he wanted now was a hot shower and a long sleep, but he couldn't because Cam needed him too. He had to find a way to explain the truth to him, why Dev hadn't been around as much lately and wouldn't be around at all in the future.

His mind was still churning over that as he stepped in the foyer to find Nancy waiting for him. She had her coat on and slung her purse over her shoulder already, obviously in a hurry to leave. "Sorry, but I need to get home. Cam's in bed. His cold's back."

Val's heart sank further, if that were possible. The day just got better and better. "Did you give him anything for it?"

"Some children's Tylenol," Nancy said as she

rushed out the door. "He's almost due for another dose."

"Thanks," he called from behind her. "Drive safely."

Once Val had locked up again for the night, he went down the hall to Cam's room. He placed a gentle hand on his son's forehead, and found it too warm.

This many infections in a row could indicate a potential problem with Cam's immune system. He frowned, wondering if he was just being a paranoid parent again, or if his medical instinct to be concerned was correct. Dev had checked him out after the last illness and found nothing wrong; he'd never ordered additional testing. Val took a deep breath and contemplated his options. Cam seemed to be doing okay now, sleeping peacefully, so the cold meds Nancy had given him seemed to be helping. She'd said he was nearly due for another dose, so that could account for the return of his fever. Without any signs of acute danger, Val decided to wait and see. Let his son sleep and reassess him in the morning. But just as Val reached the door again, a small voice behind him called out.

"Uncle Val?" Cam stirred, rolling over, his hair matted against the side of his head and his eyes sleepy.

"Hey, buddy." Val returned to the bed and sat on the edge. "Nancy said your cold's back."

"Yeah." Cam tried to sit up, but Val kept him down with a hand on his chest. "I feel yucky."

"I'm sorry, bud. But you need to rest so you'll get better." Val reached for the digital thermometer on the nightstand and held it to his son's forehead to confirm his temperature. One hundred and one. So not too worrisome.

"Is Dr. Dev here too?" Cam sniffled, looking hopeful.

Chest tight, Val brushed the hair back from the boy's flushed cheeks. He really didn't want to do this when Cam was sick, so he tried to buy himself more time to figure out what to say. "Sorry, bud. It's just you and me again tonight. How about I read you another story after you take your medicine, eh?"

"Okay," Cam replied, looking disappointed. Val knew the feeling.

Val went to grab the Tylenol from the kitchen, feeling like the weight of the world was on his shoulders. He'd weathered storms before—both in the ER and in life—but the forecast now promised turbulence ahead.

"Here you go, buddy." Val measured out a dose of the cherry-flavored syrup at Cam's bedside. "This should make you feel better."

Cam swallowed the spoonful, nose scrunched, then managed a weak smile. "Ready for my pirates."

"Pirates it is." Val grabbed the dog-eared book then settled in beside his son on the bed. "Where did we leave off?"

Hours later, Val awoke with crick in his neck from falling asleep against Cam's headboard. Early morning light streamed in through the window as he winced then straightened, glancing down at Cam, who still slept soundly, nestled beneath his covers and surrounded by pillows. The plush dinosaur toy clutched under his arm rose and fell with each congested breath, the rattling noise far too loud in the quiet room. A glance at his smartwatch said it was a little after 6:00 a.m.

Carefully, Val eased out of bed and set the book aside before crouching by the bed to gently smooth the ruffled hair away from his son's face. "Hey, buddy. How are you feeling today?"

Cam opened his eyes slowly. "A little better. Is Dr. Dev here now?"

"No. I'm afraid not." Val's throat constricted, knowing the sooner he got this over with, the better it would be for them both. Ready or not, the time had come. "Listen, Cam. Dr. Dev won't be hanging around with us anymore. I'm sorry."

"Oh." The boy looked so forlorn that Val nearly started crying himself. "Doesn't he like us anymore?"

"No, Cam. No," Val said fiercely. "He loves you."

It's me he doesn't want...

The knots in Val's stomach tightened as he took a seat on the edge of the mattress next to his son. "This is a problem between Dev and me, okay? Sometimes people just don't fit into the space we want them to. Like your Lego. You find a certain piece you think will be a perfect fit, but then you try it, and it doesn't quite work. There's nothing wrong with the pieces themselves, they just belong somewhere else. Does that make sense?"

Cam went quiet for a moment, then whispered, "Is that why Mommy left? We didn't fit her anymore?"

"Oh, buddy." Heart completely shattered now, Val held his son tight, wishing he could shield him from all the pain in the world. "Your mom never wanted to leave you, Cam. You were her perfect fit. She left because of the sickness, not you. Never you. But you know what? I think we're a perfect fit too, you and me. And no matter what happens, I'm not going anywhere. You're stuck with me, bud."

Eventually, Cam pulled back to look up at him. "Like Lego?"

"Exactly like Lego," Val said, flashing a tremulous grin.

Cam sighed. "I'll miss Dr. Dev, but as long as we're together, I'm good, Uncle Val."

"Same, buddy. Same." Val hugged his son again, holding on because that's what family did—even when the rest of the world seemed to let go.

"Will you miss Dr. Dev?" Cam asked then, driving the knife deeper into Val's chest.

He swallowed hard, glad his son couldn't see his face right then as his voice thickened. "Yes, I will."

He stayed there, holding Cam until the boy fell back to sleep, then carefully tucked him in before leaving the bedroom to make some calls. First to the ER to tell them he wouldn't be in for his shift that day, then to Nancy to give her the day off and finally to Cam's school to let them know he was home sick again. Then he refilled the humidifier in Cam's room and set it a tad higher, thinking the gentle mist would help the boy breathe easier.

Once that was done, he took a shower and

changed, then went to the kitchen to make a pot of much-needed coffee. While it was brewing, he contacted the pharmacy and scheduled a delivery of more cold medicine for Cam. He fixed himself a mug of liquid energy, then settled in the living room to figure out what their future would look like without Dev. Val still had his work and Alex, Cam had school and his activities. And speaking of Alex, he could really use a listening ear to help him work through all this. They hadn't talked since the pizza night—before everything with Dev happened—because of their crazy schedules, and he had a lot to fill his friend in on. The call rang twice before picking up.

"Hey, it's me," Val said, hearing the slight echo in the background. "Is this a bad time?"

"Good a time as any. I'm on the road, driving, as usual, between stops, so I've got a little time. You're on hands-free Bluetooth, if it sounds a little funny. What's going on?"

"I screwed up." The words tumbled out of Val in a rush of relief. It felt good to say them at last.

Alex chuckled. "I'll alert the media."

Val exhaled and scrubbed a hand over his face. "Remember Dev? I talked to you about him at pizza night?"

"The guy who texted he'd go with you to

the Timberwolves game?" Alex asked. "Yeah, I remember. You guys used to be old friends, right?"

"Well, we became a lot more than that over the next few weeks," Val said, covering his face. "We agreed up front to keep things light and uncomplicated, because he has serious trust and abandonment issues. And I said I would, but I couldn't."

"Uh-oh," Alex said, as the muted sounds of traffic filtered through in the background of the call. "Why did you agree to that, Val? You know you're basically a walking ball of emotions. Even I could see that was a bad idea a mile away, and I'm basically the poster boy for missing signs and signals."

"I know." Val groaned, sitting forward. "I was just so glad to have him around again. And I guess I was just so desperate to spend more time with him that I was willing to agree to anything." He shook his head at his own wishful thinking. "Anyway, we'd been together a few weeks, hanging out together. Cam too. Then Dev got spooked one night when Cam told him he loved him and that was basically it. He ghosted us."

"Ouch," Alex hissed. "That's harsh. What about Cam? Is he okay?"

"He's sick again, but yeah. I mean, he's sad and misses Dev, but I think he'll be okay. I want to punch Dev for hurting him though. He promised he wouldn't and then he did." Val scratched the stubble on his jaw he hadn't bothered shaving. "Of course, it was my fault too, for not being honest with Dev about how I felt for fear I'd scare him away."

Alex huffed out a breath over the line. "Wow, what a mess."

"Tell me about it," Val said, shaking his head. "Sorry to dump it all on you. I guess I just needed someone to listen and bounce ideas off of, because somehow, I have to figure this out. We still have to work together at the hospital occasionally and I don't want things to be awkward for patients. That doesn't make for good care."

After cursing under his breath, Alex said, "Hang on a sec." Several seconds passed before he returned to the line. "Sorry, had to get through some road construction. Right. How do you feel about him now? Do you still love him?"

Val gritted his teeth. Leave it to Alex to cut right to the chase. But as mad as he was at them both for this fiasco, his feelings hadn't changed where Dev was concerned. "Yeah, I do." He flopped back in his chair and pinched the bridge of his nose, eyes closed. "But I have no clue where to go from here with him."

"It's a conundrum for sure." A low whistle came from Alex's end of the call. "Well, probably the simplest solution is to talk to him about it all, like adults."

"Yeah, that's what I thought too, but it feels too soon. We just had our blowout argument last night. I can't imagine he's feeling any better about all this than I am. And I don't want him anywhere near Cam again until we work this out." He sighed and stared out the window beside him, feeling awful. "God, I'm like the worst parent ever. I finally had to tell him that Dev wouldn't be coming around anymore because he kept asking. And then he asked if it was his fault. I never want him to think that again. I told him it was like Lego. Sometimes they just don't fit like you want them to. Then he asked if Vicki left because he didn't fit her. I felt like I'd been sucker punched right in the feels. I told him that his mom loved him, and they were a perfect fit, but you never know how kids will take things…"

"Dude. First of all," Alex said over the tick-tick of his turn signal, "I have never met a person more suited for fatherhood than you, Val.

Vicki used to say the same thing. You're smart, caring, kind, empathetic, funny. Cam couldn't ask for a better parent than you. And second, sometimes you have to make hard decisions and do things even when the timing isn't the greatest. That's life. I'm sure it wasn't easy to tell Cam that, but you did it. Wait a little while if you think you need to, then talk to this Dev guy and be honest with him. I mean, what's the worst that could happen? He can't leave you again, right?"

"No, I guess not." Val slumped farther down in his seat, sadness moving like sludge through his body. "I just feel horrible about everything. We were friends long before we slept together. I should never have lied to him, Alex. Especially after what happened with his ex-husband. And he lost his dad too, when he was about Cam's age. Just walked out on him and his mom. So Dev comes by his trust issues honestly. And then I go and basically lie right to his face again just to keep sleeping with him." He covered his eyes. "I called him an emotionless, careless bastard."

"Well, it sounds like maybe he might have deserved it." Alex took a deep breath and the sound of his engine cutting off sounded over the phone. "I just pulled into the lot for my next appointment, so I have to go, but listen, whatever you said or did, it takes two people to screw up a relationship. Him walking out on you and Cam without a word like that sounds like he's to blame in all this too, yeah? I think it all comes down to that conversation you need to have with him."

Val nodded and took a deep breath. "You're right. I need to talk to Dev. Thanks for confirming it."

"Sure thing." Alex's smile was evident in his voice. "Let me know how it goes."

"Will do." Val grinned. "Now go sell some drugs."

After the call ended, Val sat with his coffee and stared out the window beside him, needing to think about what he'd say to Dev once he finally set up a time to talk.

CHAPTER NINE

IN THE FOUR DAYS since his fight with Val, Dev had taken to running at dawn, the crisp Minneapolis air biting at his cheeks as he wove through the still-sleeping neighborhood where he'd grown up. In these solitary moments, with his breath clouding the air and the rhythmic thud of his sneakers against the pavement, he found a fleeting peace—a respite from the mess he'd created.

Today, he'd inadvertently left his phone back at the house instead of tucking it in the pocket of his running jacket like usual, but it was probably for the best. Saved him from checking it a billion times to see if there was a call or text from Val. Which was beyond pathetic. Because why would he contact Dev? Their argument in the break room had been a definitive ending.

An emotionless, careless bastard...

That's what Val had called him, and as much as it pained him to admit, it was probably true.

Stuffing down his feelings and getting on with life was how Dev dealt with things. It was how he'd survived after his father had left and again when Tom had betrayed him, but now it seemed he was doing it all the time. And when he'd spent those few blissful weeks with Val and Cam and the walls inside had started to crack and crumble, that's when he'd panicked.

God, I really am a bastard.

Loneliness continued to dog his heels all the way home, through his shower and getting dressed, to the kitchen where he found his mother waiting for him at the table. He got his coffee, intending to sit in the living room to check his emails, but she caught his arm as he passed by.

"Wait, honey. Come sit with me for a second. Tell me what's wrong."

He couldn't look at her as he took a seat across from her, staring at the quilt draped over the back of the sofa just past her shoulder instead, his eyes tracing the patchwork of cloth as she waited.

Eventually, her motherly concern won him over, and Dev huffed out a breath, the tension inside him deflating as his stoic facade vanished, replaced by abject sadness. He ended up pouring out the whole story to her: his reunion with Val, their friendship crossing the line into something more, his decision to walk away and why. When he finished, he felt hollowed out, empty, for the first time in months.

"Oh, sweetie." She took his hand. "You really screwed up."

He snorted, and finally hazarded a glance at his mom, feelings raw. "I know. And the worst part is, I thought I was helping. It seems like I've spent every day of my life since Dad left us waiting for the other shoe to drop. Fearing everything good would disappear without warning." He gave a sad little shrug. "For a long time growing up, I wondered if him abandoning us was my fault somehow. Like if I'd just been a better kid, a more perfect son, he would have stayed. I wondered the same thing after Tom and I split up too. Thinking if I'd just done better, been better, he wouldn't have strayed." Dev shook his head, staring down at the black coffee in his cup. "Burying my emotions became easier for me. It felt safer not feeling anything, pushing it all down and locking it away. I felt more in control. But when Val reappeared in my life, it was like that control went out the window. Suddenly, I was feeling everything again and it was overwhelming and confusing. Terrifying, if I'm truthful. And the more time

I spent with him and Cam together, the more it felt right. Which only made all those doubts and fears and anxieties I'd pushed aside return twice as strong later. And once I realized what had happened to me, that all my barriers were gone, my sense of impending doom grew to the point where I felt like the best decision I could make to keep us all safe was to remove myself from the situation entirely. Because even though I'd vowed not to, I love Val. Cam too." He hung his head and squeezed his eyes shut, ashamed. "So I left. To protect all of us from future heartache. I told myself it was for their own good. But in reality, I was just running away from the best thing that had ever happened to me. How messed up is that?"

"Honey." His mother took his hand. "Listen to me, please. Your father leaving never had anything to do with you. He had one foot out the door long before you were born. And I'm sorry you lived all these years thinking differently. I wish you'd told me you felt that way."

Dev managed a nod, eyes stinging as he focused on the tabletop, not trusting his voice.

"And as to you and Val, it does sound like you've gotten yourself into a pickle there, that's for sure. Trust is a tricky thing. Once you lose it, it's hard to get back. You have to earn it.

And while I know you're scared by what you feel for him and his son—" her thumb brushed against his knuckles as she talked, a comforting rhythm that lulled him into relaxing for the first time in days "—that doesn't mean it isn't real or right. And it doesn't mean that you should give up either. Talk to Val. Tell him how you feel. Val isn't Tom. He isn't your father either. And he's been through his own pain these last few years. I think both of you need each other more than ever. You're good together. You understand each other. And that little boy loves you both so much. Show them that you can and will be there for them going forward. Show them the courage I know you have inside you. Real courage this time, the kind that comes from your heart and soul and isn't afraid to feel and love because, in the end, that's the only truth there is."

Dev looked into his mother's eyes at last, two wells of wisdom and understanding that seemed to see right into his soul. She knew everything there was to know about him, had guided him through scraped knees and broken hearts, through academic pressures and professional challenges. She knew his best and his worst, and she still loved and supported him, just like Val had always done. His heart swelled in his chest until it felt like it would burst. "I want to make a family with them."

"That's wonderful, honey." She smiled. "All the more reason to talk to Val as soon as possible. Tell him what you just told me. No risk, no reward. Love—the real kind—isn't easy, but it's so worth it."

Dev nodded, then asked, "Did you hate Dad for leaving us?"

She shrugged. "Maybe a little, at first. But after a while, I realized it was for the best. Hard as it was raising you on my own, I think we were better off just the two of us, eh?"

He chuckled. "Agreed."

"Good." She grinned. "Now, go win back the man you love and his kid."

The warmth of his mother's unwavering faith in him seemed to shift something inside Dev. Her words didn't erase his insecurities, but they did remind him he wasn't alone. And maybe, just maybe, that was enough for him to mend fences and start moving forward again.

"Okay…" His voice caught slightly, and he cleared his throat. "I worried after Tom that I'd never heal, never find someone again, but I did. Right here where I started. Funny how that happens, huh?"

"Yes." His mom smiled as Dev continued

processing everything that had happened to him since returning to his hometown. If anything, Val and Cam had taught him how to embrace life fully again. He yearned to be back at their sides and show them both they could depend on him, that he'd be there from this day forward, to beg for forgiveness and another chance to show them exactly how steadfast he could be.

"But honestly," his mother continued. "I was surprised you two didn't end up together all those years ago. Never seen two people so compatible with each other before. Then that idiot Tom swept you off your feet. All I can say is I'm glad you're back, honey, and I'm glad you've found your true home at last." She squeezed his hand once more then let him go. "Now, go and prove to Val and Cam why they can't live without you. And before you go driving yourself nuts, remember they don't need perfection. They just need you, Dev. All of you, even the imperfect parts that are still healing."

Dev nodded, knowing it was true. The possibility of loss and disappointment and hurt would always be there, lurking at the edges of life, but so was the possibility of something real and lasting and true. Love wasn't guaranteed or was forever, but perhaps the risk made it even sweeter.

As he grabbed his coat, he felt a new determination. The path forward wouldn't be easy, but he was no longer willing to allow the specter of past pain to dictate his future steps. He opened the front door, then paused. "Wish me luck, Mom."

"You don't need luck, honey," she called as he stepped outside into the brisk late autumn day. "You got this!"

The air hinted at the coming winter, but inside, Dev burned with the warmth of renewed purpose. With each step toward his car, his apprehension lifted a bit more. His mother was right. Val and Cam deserved all the parts of him—the good, the bad and the in-between—and everything he had to give. Before, he would've done everything in his power to hide the sides of himself he felt were broken, unworthy, unlovable. He would've kept his emotions under wraps and tried to logic his way out of it. But logic was what had gotten him into this mess. Now it was time to listen to his heart.

By the time he reached the medical center, he was brimming with determination to find Val and talk to him. Opportunity soon presented itself when he was paged down to the ER for a consult. There was no requesting physician listed in the text, so it was possible it wasn't Val, but still, it would put them in the same department and Dev could seek him out from there. He rode the elevator down to the first floor, squaring his shoulders as he stepped off and headed toward the busy nurses' station, determined to get it all out in the open with Val. "Dr. Harrison. I was paged for a consult."

"That was me." That familiar voice sent his pulse racing like a thoroughbred. Val. "It's my patient."

Dev turned slowly, feeling like every eye in the department was watching him, apprehension prickling his cheeks as nervous heat climbed from beneath the collar of his dress shirt. Thankfully, Val acted normally, handing Dev a tablet with the chart pulled up on it as they walked toward the trauma bays. He gave the rundown. "Twelve-year-old female patient with abnormal levels of serum tumor markers and liver function in the serology. Ultrasound imaging revealed a large mass in the left lobe of the liver. No lesions elsewhere."

"Symptoms?" Dev asked, his voice gruffer than usual as he studied the lab results. They would talk. He'd find the time, but first they had a patient to treat, and they both had to focus on that.

"None. But from what I read, that's not unusual in some cases." Val opened a curtain to reveal a girl named Maria with large brown eyes peering out from a too-pale face beneath a dark mop of hair. "This is Dr. Harrison, pediatric oncologist. I've called him in for a consult."

Dev proceeded to introduce himself to the patient and her parents, then performed his own exam, palpating the patient's abdomen, aware of Val on the other side of the bed, watching him. He asked Maria, "Does this hurt when I press here?" Then to her parents when Maria winced and nodded, he asked, "How is her appetite?"

"Fine, I think," the mother said. "What's wrong with her?"

"That's what we're hoping to discover," Dev said, removing his gloves and tossing them in a nearby biohazard bin before washing his hands. "The ultrasound showed a mass on her liver, so I'd like to get a biopsy of that. The diagnosis will depend on those findings."

After getting their consent for the procedure and explaining it all to both parents and his new patient, Dev followed Val out of the exam room, speaking low to avoid being overheard. "Based on my exam, I'd guess we're dealing with a rhabdomyosarcoma, but I'll still need that biopsy to confirm."

Val grimaced as they arrived back at the

nurses' station. "The prognosis isn't great for that type."

"No, but there are new treatments available and several clinical trials for new drugs she might qualify for. We'll see once we know exactly what we're dealing with."

They both stood there then, staring at each other. Dev suddenly tongue-tied now that the moment had arrived, his adrenaline skyrocketing. He could do this. He would do this. He swallowed hard, then said, "Val, I…" at the same time Val said, "Dev, I…"

"Dr. Laurent?" one of the nurses called from across the corridor. "You're needed in trauma bay two, stat!"

Val gave Dev an apologetic look as he backed away. "Sorry, I have to go. We'll talk later. Let me know when those labs come in."

Dev watched him walk away, feeling disappointed. Mainly in himself for not going for it when he'd had a chance. As he headed back upstairs, he thought Val had looked tired, his blue eyes shadowed, and wondered if he'd had trouble sleeping too. Dev had woken up last night, reaching for a warm body beside him that wasn't there.

We'll talk later, Val had said.

For Dev, later couldn't come soon enough.

* * *

Once the lab results were back, Dev headed back down to the ER to discuss treatment plans with Val instead of calling, hoping that after they met with the patient, they might have a chance to talk privately. Maria's diagnosis was as he'd expected. Rhabdomyosarcoma, a type of cancer that starts in the growth cells of soft tissue, like muscles and tendons, but can spread quickly to other parts of the body, which is most likely how it had ended up on Maria's liver.

He and Val stood shoulder to shoulder now in front of an ER computer screen, staring at the images.

"So, what's the treatment plan?" Val asked, arms crossed.

"We'll need to be aggressive, since it's already metastasized," Dev said. "Surgery to remove as much of the liver mass as possible. Then, once she's recovered from that procedure, chemotherapy and radiation for at least the next fifteen months. Agreed?"

"You're the expert," Val said, giving Dev some side-eye. "Listen, about that talk, I—"

"Code blue! Code blue! Trauma bay two! All available ER personnel required!" blared over the PA system and people began racing to the scene. Val swore under his breath, looking frustrated. "Sorry. You'll have to talk to Maria and her family yourself, I guess. Text me later about that talk."

Then he hurried off to his next emergency.

Gah!

Dev was starting to think there was some cosmic conspiracy to prevent him from telling Val that he loved him. He vowed next time they saw each other, he'd come right out with it, no matter what else was happening.

When he'd finished saving the code blue gunshot victim, who had gone into cardiac arrest, Val came out of the trauma bay hoping to find Dev waiting for him, but of course he wasn't. The man was busy too with his own patients to see, so it was silly to expect Dev to be standing around, waiting to talk to him.

He went back to the nurses' station to see if there was anyone waiting to be seen. Keeping busy would help make the last hour of his shift go faster. Before he grabbed a new chart, he pulled out his phone to send Dev a quick text to ask him if he was available later that night to talk and to text him a time. But before he sent it, his phone vibrated with an incoming call. His stomach bottomed out when Nancy's face appeared. It had to be serious enough for Nancy to call during his shift. He stepped off to the side of the corridor for privacy then answered. "What's wrong?"

"His fever came back a few hours ago. One hundred and one. So I gave him the cold meds, like you said, but then he started vomiting. I got him cleaned up from that but now I can't wake him up!" Nancy said, her tone panicked. "I called 911. They're here now and we're heading to the medical center."

Val's world slowed to a halt, his insides going into a full parental fear meltdown. Yes, he was a doctor himself. No, it didn't matter when it was your own child. He felt frantic and desperate to help his son in any way he could as quickly as possible.

The next twenty minutes were agony as he monitored the call-board and waited for Cam's arrival. According to the reports Nancy was giving as she rode alongside the paramedics in the ambulance, Cam's fever had now spiked to one hundred and four, and his breathing was shallow and strained, only interrupted by occasional wet, rough coughs. Cam had also moaned like he was in pain when the paramedics stabilized his neck on the gurney, and in one exam he displayed photosensitivity. Val's years of medical training pointed to a diagnosis that terrified him.

Meningitis.

He checked the hospital records for any reports of recent local outbreaks of bacterial meningitis, but couldn't find any. It didn't mean it wasn't the culprit though. The potentially lethal infection, which caused swelling of the brain and spinal cord, could also be caused by certain viruses and some fungi too. And the sooner Cam received treatment, the better. It could make the difference between a favorable outcome and...

No. He would not go there. Could not go there.

Cam would get through this. Had to get through this.

Val glanced up at the clock on the wall above him and wondered what the hell was taking them so long as he paced the floor of the ER in front of the ambulance bay, each minute elongating until his nerves were stretched taut.

Finally, after what felt like a small eternity, the ambulance finally arrived, and though he was forbidden to treat his own family members, Val still raced out to meet them as a concerned father. Poor Cam looked so small and helpless strapped to the gurney the paramedics rushed through the automatic doors, the boy's complexion gray except for the bright pink flush across his cheeks. An oxygen mask covered his nose and mouth, and he was unresponsive, though the paramedics assured him Cam had a steady, strong pulse.

Nancy was a wreck too, crying and shaking. She kept apologizing to Val like it was her fault, but he assured her it wasn't. She went to sit in the waiting room to wait for news, saying her husband was going to join her, so she wouldn't be alone while Val stayed with his son.

"Cam, buddy?" Val held his hand as he hurried alongside the gurney toward one of the special isolation trauma bays in the ER. They were taking special precautions to prevent spread of any infection until they had a confirmed diagnosis. Cam's eyes remained stubbornly closed, despite Val trying to rouse him. "I'm right here, Cam. You're going to be okay. Just stay with me, buddy. We'll make it through this."

Once they reached the assigned room, staff in special personal protective equipment rushed Cam inside then closed the door on Val, leaving him outside to peer in through the glass window as his whole life fought to survive on that gurney.

He'd promised himself, promised Vicki, that he'd always protect Cam. He could not fail now.

That evening, Dev returned to the ER to make sure he'd tied up all the loose ends for Maria's case before he left for the night. After their second foiled attempt to talk, Dev had sent Val a text asking if he had time for a drink after work. That was over three hours ago, and he still hadn't gotten a response. Not that that meant anything. Given how busy Val had been earlier, he could still be tied up with patients. He missed talking to Val, not just about work but about anything. And he longed to spend time with Cam again too, talking about his models or his latest soccer game. Anything, really…

He rode the elevator down to the first floor, resisting the urge to rub the sore spot over his heart. It had been there since seeing Val earlier, and was purely from loneliness and yearning.

He'd been so determined to keep to himself, keep his heart safe after the brutal betrayal by Tom. And yet, Val and Cam had both gotten around his barriers with their joy and laughter and sweet smiles. With their sunshine and hope. And now Dev couldn't live without it— without them—again.

By the time he arrived on the first floor, Dev had checked his phone again. Still nothing.

The elevator dinged and the door whooshed open to another brightly lit hall, and Dev stepped off thinking maybe after he was done with Maria's file, he'd just try to find Val again in person.

CHAPTER TEN

VAL SAT OUT in the hallway, anxiously awaiting any news about Cam and checking his smartwatch constantly. Three hours had passed and still no news, other than Cam was stable and still unconscious. Several of his ER colleagues had passed by on their way to other patients, all of them giving him sympathetic glances and encouraging pats on the shoulder. And while Val appreciated their concern, none of it made him feel any better.

Each time the door to Cam's room opened, Val's heart jumped and he stood, hoping for a new update, some good news. But as yet another specialist went into Cam's room, Val sank back into his seat, despondent. This must be how his ER patients felt when they brought in their loved ones for emergencies. Being on the other side of things from his usual perspective as the physician in charge was not fun. He wanted to charge in there and demand answers, but knew they needed to concentrate on his son right now, so he stayed put. Nancy and her husband had come back a couple of times to check on him and on Cam, but Val hadn't had much to tell them, and they'd both looked dead on their feet, so he'd told them to go on home with a promise he'd let them know as soon as he found out anything new.

He wished Dev was there to lend advice, or just be a warm presence for support. He finally got a chance to check his phone and saw a text from Dev asking if he wanted to get a drink. But they hadn't had their talk yet, and Val was exhausted, so adding alcohol to that mix probably wasn't a great idea at that point. Besides, he planned to stick close to his son's bedside until he was well again, so...

"Please," he prayed to whoever might be listening, including Vicki. "Let him be okay."

But Val knew Cam was in the best hands now. He worked with these people every day, and there was no medical team he trusted more to care for his son at this critical time. That was something at least.

He dragged a hand through his hair for the umpteenth time, then stood again, too restless to just sit there anymore, so he paced the hall for a bit before wandering down to the public waiting room out front. He stood at the windows, staring out at the glittering city lights of Minneapolis and beyond, seeking some solace or distraction from the nightmare his present reality had become.

As his initial burst of adrenaline from the ambulance's arrival earlier ebbed away, it left soul-draining exhaustion in its wake. Maybe Dev was still here. He could go up to his office and check, but didn't want to leave the ER in case something changed with Cam. So, finally, he sat down again, resting his head back against the chair and closing his eyes, memories of their day at the park filling his head. Cam's laughter as he'd played basketball with Dev or threw the Frisbee. Cam and Dev building Lego sets together, constructing new worlds from colorful bricks. The three of them eating ice cream, watching movies, doing everyday normal things that families did all the time. But every happy recollection now felt like a shard of glass, beautiful but painful, a sharp reminder of what he was fighting to get back...

"Come on, Cam," he whispered. "Beat this like I know you can."

When Val opened his eyes again, the clock on the wall in front of him ticked with maddening slowness, each second a drop of water in an empty bucket. He leaned forward, elbows on knees, head cradled in hands, willing things to move faster, for the team to find a diagnosis so they could begin treatment. What was taking so long? Had Cam gotten worse? Had he died in there and no one told him?

Then, as if summoned by him, the automatic doors leading into the ER finally opened and out walked one of the specialists—Fred, who'd been working on his son. He took a seat beside Val to explain the situation. "We're doing everything we can to narrow it down precisely so we can treat him the most effectively, but it's leaning toward viral meningitis. We'll need the lumbar puncture to confirm and type it, and I put a stat rush on the labs. But he's stable and holding his own, though he hasn't regained consciousness yet."

Val dug the heels of his hands into his scratchy eyes. Viral meningitis was the most common type in children, and the least lethal. It was easier to treat too and less contagious. With his recent spate of colds and sinus infections, Cam would've been more susceptible to it also. All the pieces fell into place. "Can I see him?"

Fred stood and clapped a hand on his shoulder. "You can. I'll let you know as soon as we get the results back."

"Thanks, Fred." Val stood to follow him back into the ER, Vicki's last words echoing in his mind.

Take care of Cam for me.

Her final plea, his final promise.

I'm trying, sis. I'm trying.

Dev froze in his tracks halfway to the nurses' station because of what he saw on the patient board—Cam's name and words *suspected viral meningitis.*

What the—

Heart lodged in his throat, he grabbed a tablet and typed in Cam's name to pull up the file. It looked like they'd already run a litany of tests, including a lumbar puncture to precisely type the virus involved, but they'd already started him on IV antiviral meds and steroids to help reduce the inflammation in Cam's body.

Oh, boy.

Val must be sick with worry. Dev checked the file again and saw that they were going to move him up to the PICU once a bed opened up, but until then he was still here in the ER, in a special isolation room. Dev hurried toward it, Cam's last words to him chasing at his heels.

Good night, Dr. Dev... I love you...

He stopped outside the door and looked

through the glass to see Val at his son's bedside, hair disheveled, his blue eyes dulled by fatigue and worry as he held the hand of an unconscious Cam, who looked far too small in that great big hospital bed.

Then Val looked over, as if sensing him there, and Dev went inside, words bubbling up inside him and clamoring to get out.

I'm sorry. I'm here for you. I love you, Val. I love you too, Cam.

He placed a hand on Val's shoulder and Val reached up to cover it with his own, a small sign of solidarity that helped ease the tension a bit. "I just found out, or I would've been down here sooner. Has there been any change in his condition? I looked up his file."

"No. Not yet." Val watched his son as he spoke. "He hasn't woken up since they brought him in."

"I'm sorry." Dev cursed quietly under his breath. He hated feeling helpless, but knew they were doing everything they could at present.

"I can't lose him," Val said raggedly, tears running down his cheeks.

Dev pulled Val up then and into his arms, offering whatever comfort he could. "It's okay. I'm here. Cam's going to be okay. They're giving him the best care possible."

"I know," Val mumbled, eventually gathering himself and pulling away. "I'm sorry to fall apart on you. I just hate the fact that I didn't see this coming sooner."

"How could you?" Dev said, pulling up a chair beside him. "You know as well as I do that the symptoms often start out mild and can turn severe without warning. Like you said before, those classrooms are petri dishes of infection. No telling where he might have picked it up. And most times, it never even manifests to this degree. There's no way you could have predicted this. Don't blame yourself."

Finally, Val nodded. "Thanks for saying that. And thanks for being here with us now."

Dev took Val's hand and shifted to look him in the eye. "I'll always be here for you and Cam, Val. If you'll forgive me. I was such an idiot before and I'm sorry. About everything."

Before he could say more, a nurse stuck his head in to say, "Val, a bed opened in the PICU, so they'll be moving him upstairs now. We're all optimistic that he'll make a full recovery."

"Thanks," Val said. "Me too."

The nurse left as orderlies came in to start moving Cam up to the PICU. Val walked out into the hall and gestured for Dev to follow. Once they'd found a relatively private alcove, he turned to Dev and said, "Thank you for being here and for the apology. And I want you to know I'm sorry too."

"About what?" Dev said, frowning.

"I broke our agreement."

Dev blinked at him. "How?"

Val sighed and shook his head. "We'd agreed to keep things uncomplicated, light. I tried, Dev. I really did, but I couldn't do it. I know you're scared to love, but I can't help myself where you're concerned. I fell in love with you, and I was afraid to tell you because I wanted more time with you. So, I lied. And I'm so sorry."

It took a minute for Dev to process what he had said, and once he did, he couldn't help the relieved laugh that came out of him. They'd been dancing around the truth when it was right there in front of them all the time, if only they'd been brave enough to see it and say it.

Val's brows knitted together. "This is funny to you?"

"What? No." Dev sobered, though he couldn't stop his smile. "It's just that I love you too, Val, but I was too terrified to tell you. Hell, I was too terrified even to admit it to myself for too long. That's why I left. I thought distance would make it go away on its own, but it didn't."

"Love isn't a disease, Dev." Val gave him a

look. "It's okay to have feelings. They're normal."

"I know." He stared down at his hands in his lap. "But after what I'd been through, they also felt toxic. I didn't want to get hurt again, so it seemed better to not have them."

"And how did that work out for you?" Val raised a brow at him, his tone dripping with snark.

Yeah, he deserved that, Dev supposed, after walking away from the best thing that had ever happened to him. Not once, but twice. But now that they were putting it all out there, he needed to say his piece to be able to move forward. "I want to apologize to you properly. All of this was my fault. At the time, leaving seemed like the best way to protect all of us from being hurt, but I only made things worse. That's not an excuse for my behavior, but I wanted you to understand my thinking. My leaving had nothing to do with you or Cam. I love you both more than I can say, and I'm never going to leave again, unless you ask me to. Promise."

Val leaned over to rest his head on Dev's shoulder as Dev took a deep breath then continued.

"I've been trying to hide my feelings since my dad left, thinking that was how I could keep myself from ever getting hurt like that again. I know how ridiculous that sounds, but I was five and that's how kids think. Anyway, that's when I decided that locking my emotions away was the key to safety, and the easiest way to do that was to be alone. Keep everything under wraps, lock it down so I wouldn't be hurt again when things ended or people left, because in my experience, they always did. I had my mom, and then I had you, and I thought that was all I needed. Then Tom blew into my life like a hurricane and knocked me off my feet. For the first time in what felt like forever, I thought maybe, finally, I could try again. But I was wrong, and things fell apart once more, and to me, that just proved my point. Don't let anything show. Don't let people in. Otherwise, you'll get hurt. After we separated, the pain was too real, too raw, dividing up our lives like the weekly recycling. I shut down all my emotions again. Then I came back here and saw you on my first day, reminding me of what I'd left behind—true friendship and belonging and real love and caring—and I reinforced my walls and made them even higher and sturdier. But even then, somehow, you and Cam got around them before I even knew what was happening. And once I did realize how far gone I was, I panicked and ran away. Like an idiot…" He cleared the lump from his throat. "But I'm done running. I love you, Val. I think I always did. Even back in medical school. Which means I broke our agreement way before you, so you had nothing to lie about because our agreement was already void. I love Cam too. And I know what I did hurt you both, and I can't guarantee I won't screw up again at some point because, well, I'm a broken toy. A real mess. That's the truth. And you of all people should know that. I carry a lot of baggage, and I'm not always the easiest person to deal with. I can be stubborn and opinionated and a real pain in the ass. But if you're willing to give it a go, so am I. You've seen me at my worst and at my best, and you're still here. That means so much to me. More than I can say. I love you, Valentine Laurent, and I want to be yours forever, if you'll have me."

Val didn't respond, and as a beat passed, then two, Dev's heart sank. That's when the nervous babbling started.

"I totally understand if you're done, Val. And I'll respect your wishes if you never want to see me again. I failed you when you needed me most. But I'd like to make amends, if you'll let me. Prove to you that you can trust me with your heart. I want to move forward, Val, and I hope we can do that together."

Finally, Val lifted his head, took Dev's face in his hands, and kissed Dev soundly on the lips. When they finally pulled apart, his blue eyes were bright as stars. "Of course I forgive you, you infuriating man. I've loved you from the first moment I saw you sitting alone in the corner of that classroom at the beginning of medical school. I thought you were the sexiest nerd on campus. And I love you even more now."

They hugged then, Dev not sure how he'd gotten so lucky, but so grateful anyway. "I meant what I said too. I plan to spend every day from now on proving to you and Cam that I'll be there for you both." He leaned his forehead against Val's. "For as long as you'll have me."

"Forever," Val murmured against his neck, holding Dev like he'd never let him go again. "That's how long I want you with us."

After following the medical entourage up to Cam's new room, they took up their posts beside his bed, and Dev couldn't help glancing over periodically to confirm that Val was still there, not quite believing it yet. He'd done it. He'd been brave, he'd followed his heart and emotions, and it had worked out. Imagine that. Once they'd both settled in at Cam's bedside, they napped in rotation in case someone came in with an update. When it was Dev's turn after midnight, it felt like he'd just closed his eyes, but when he opened them again, early morning sunlight was streaming in through the window behind Val, highlighting his tawny hair and giving him an almost ethereal glow. Even rumpled and sleep-deprived, he was still the handsomest man Dev had ever seen. His palms itched to touch Val, hold him, but that could come later.

First, they had to get Cam well again.

Then Val looked over at him and Dev's heart thumped hard, whatever remnants left of his inner walls vanishing completely, allowing Val to see him—all of him—even though it terrified Dev. Then Val smiled, and Dev knew it would be all right. Whatever challenges the future threw their way, they'd handle it. Together.

Val finally broke the connection by turning his attention to Cam and taking the boy's limp hand as a nurse came in to check on the IVs. Hopefully, they'd see some sign of improvement in him soon.

Around noon, Val watched as the nurse fiddled with Cam's IVs and Dev got up to stretch his legs. Various medical staff had come in like clockwork about every twenty minutes to reassess his son's condition, but so far, all Val had received from them were platitudes and pitying looks. He and Vicki had gotten enough of those as growing up poor kids with deadbeat parents. Then, after his sister's funeral, he'd gotten more of the same. At least then, he'd been so wrapped up in helping Cam adjust to his new life that Val hadn't had time to notice. Now though, it felt suffocating. The only thing that made this weight bearable was Dev. Knowing that they were okay, that they were in love and would have a future together gave him a bright spot to focus on amongst the darkness. He needed that more than he could say.

The nurse left, and Dev waved him over to the computer in the corner of the room where he'd brought up Cam's file. "Val, come look at this."

Val walked around his son's bed to see the screen, taking strength from the other man's warmth. "What?"

"From the counts, it looks like the drugs are starting to work," Dev said, pointing to the most recent set of blood work drawn shortly after Cam had arrived in the PICU.

"Let's hope that continues," Val said, forcing himself to stay grounded. While his son's condition hadn't gotten any worse since he'd been in the hospital, it hadn't gotten noticeably better either. But Val was counting his blessings where he could. And having Dev's support in his hour of need helped.

He sat again and took his son's hand, warming Cam's small, chilled fingers with his own larger ones. "Come on, buddy. You can do this. Come back to us."

Val then proceeded to tell Cam what was happening, even though the boy gave no sign of hearing him. There'd been many studies that said unconscious patients could still hear and understand voices around them, and it made Val feel better to pretend things were normal anyway, even if they weren't. That's when he felt Cam squeeze his fingers ever so slightly. His heart stumbled and his eyes widened. His son was still there, still fighting. "That's it, Cam. Come back to me, buddy. Can you open your eyes? Please."

Dev rushed to the other side of the bed. "What happened?"

"He squeezed my hand," Val said, throat constricting and eyes stinging. "I think he's coming around."

"Yes!" Dev took Cam's other hand. "Hey, Cam. It's Dr. Dev. I'm here with you and your dad. I've missed you so much, and I'm so sorry

I haven't been there these last few weeks. But I'm back and I'm not leaving again, I promise."

It took a few seconds, but soon Cam's fingers tightened around Dev's hand too. "I felt it!"

Val couldn't hide his grin as fresh tears fell down his cheeks. "He's going to be okay."

"Yes, he's going to be okay," Dev repeated, flashing Val a watery smile in return. "He's waking up."

Sure enough, Cam's eyelids fluttered before slowly opening enough to reveal the clear blue irises Val had longed to see again, his son's expression a mix of confusion and weariness. "Wh-what's h-happening?" Cam croaked out. "Wh-where am I?"

Val kissed Cam's hand, his tone laced with relief and joy. "Hey there, buddy."

Dev grinned down at Cam from the other side of the bed. "Welcome back."

"Uncle Val? Wh-why are you c-crying?" Cam's gaze darted between them. "Dr. Dev?"

"You've been really sick," Val said, his words rough with emotion as he kissed his son's forehead. "You scared me."

"S-sorry," Cam said, a hint of his usual mischievousness returning.

"It's okay, buddy." Val ruffled Cam's tawny

hair affectionately. "Just know we both love you so much."

"How are you feeling now, Cam?" Dev asked.

"Better." Cam's voice grew stronger the longer he talked until the stutter disappeared. Another good sign. "Does this mean you'll come over to see me again, Dr. Dev?"

"I absolutely will," Dev said. "In fact, I'll be there so much, you might get tired of seeing me."

Cam's smile widened. "Yay!"

"Okay," Val said, glancing at the monitors. "We'll let you get some more rest."

"And we'll be here when you wake up again," Dev reassured him.

"Promise?" Cam asked, his eyelids drooping as his limited energy waned once more.

"Promise," both men affirmed in unison.

Once Cam drifted off, they remained at the bedside, Val feeling like he was home, even in this stressful environment, because the people he loved were there. Eventually, when he was sure Cam was doing better, he reluctantly agreed to leave so he could shower and change and maybe take a power nap. Or a thousand.

Dev said he'd drive, since Val felt ready to drop and didn't trust himself behind the wheel.

As they waited for an elevator, Dev brushed

a stray lock of unruly hair from Val's forehead. "Thank you for giving me another chance. And thank you for letting me be part of your family."

The elevator dinged and both men walked into the empty car. Once the doors closed, Val wrapped his arms around Dev, pulling him close. "Thank you for wanting to be a part of it."

Once they were outside in the physician's parking lot, Val winced. "Man, I need a shower."

"Yes, you do," Dev teased gently, a hint of much-needed humor creeping into his tone.

Val winked at him over the hood of the gray sedan. "I also need to eat, so maybe you could fix us some food while I take care of business. I'm starving."

As Val climbed into the passenger seat and Dev got behind the wheel, it felt like a huge weight had finally lifted. The days ahead were looking brighter with each passing second.

CHAPTER ELEVEN

Three weeks later...

DEV ADJUSTED HIS GLASSES and smiled.

I can't believe I'm back here again.

"Look at it! Isn't it cool?" Cam's eyes were as wide as saucers, his finger tracing the picture of the spacecraft on the box for his new NASA Artemis Space Launch System Lego set with reverence. "We can build it together, Dev!"

Val beamed at them from the open kitchen, his expression a mix of pride and deep affection.

"Yes, we can," Dev agreed, taking a seat on the floor and ruffling Cam's hair. "We'll make it the best spaceship ever."

They opened the box and spread out the colorful Lego blocks across the living room floor, creating a galaxy of tiny plastic components that awaited their transformation. The afternoon light filtered through the window, casting a warm glow over the scene. Cam sat cross-legged with an instruction booklet in his lap, scanning the pages with eager anticipation.

"How about we start with the base?" Dev asked, picking up a gray piece and examining it closely before picking up a second piece that looked like it might fit and trying them together.

Cam shook his head, grabbing a different piece, snapping them together perfectly. "It goes like this."

Together, they assembled the launchpad, clicking each intricate piece into place with satisfying snaps. The activity was meditative, and Dev soon lost himself in it, his analytical brain overjoyed.

"Dev?" Cam's voice pulled him from his thoughts, quieter now, contemplative. The boy looked up at him, his hair falling into his eyes. "Are you going to stay forever this time?"

Dev's heart swelled with sweetness. Since Cam had been discharged from the hospital three days after he'd entered it, Dev had all but moved into their house, only going back to his mom's a couple of times a week to check on her. Eventually, they planned to sell both houses and buy a bigger one with a guest suite that would accommodate all four of them—

Cam, Val, Dev and his mom. "I will, if that's okay with you."

"It's great!" Cam said, working a little slower now as he attached a cylindrical piece to the base before looking up again. "Are you going to be my second dad?"

Dev's steady hands faltered slightly as he tried adding another section to the structure. He and Val had discussed marriage—if they wanted to get married or not. And while they weren't rushing into anything, it was a possibility at some point. For now, they were just savoring every day together. "Would you like me to be your second dad?"

"I would!" Cam said, a grin lighting up his face. It was the kind of smile that could turn a room from ordinary to extraordinary, and reminded Dev again of why he'd chosen pediatrics in the first place: to protect those smiles, to fight for them when the darkness threatened to swallow them whole. Cam was doing well, post-meningitis. In fact, Cam had been lucky, with no lasting issues from the disease. "You give me bigger ice-cream scoops than Uncle Val."

"Ask a silly question," Val chimed in from the kitchen.

"I know," Dev laughed. The kid deserved

the biggest scoops he could handle. "Serves me right."

They fell into an easy silence then, Dev and Cam building, while Val made lasagna for dinner using his sister's recipe.

"There's an air and space museum in Ohio. Maybe next summer, we can take a trip there to see the planes and rockets," Dev said, thinking aloud as he connected another section of scaffolding to the model. "If you'd like that."

"Yes! I'd love that!" Cam's blue eyes lit up as he called to Val, "Did you hear, Uncle Val? We're going to the space museum next year! Maybe I can learn more about the stars before then. Like those big balls of gas burning billions of miles away from the book you read to me in the hospital!"

Val chuckled as he shoved the lasagna in the oven, then joined them in the living room and sank into a seat on the sofa. "Sounds like a plan, buddy."

As they continued assembling the Lego set, Cam added, "I love you, Dev."

Dev glanced at Val, his heart nearly bursting. "I love you too, Cam."

From the sofa, Val smiled, knowing what they'd been through to get there, and looking as grateful as Dev felt to have it at last—to have

Cam home and healthy, and the new family they'd formed. An affirmation of their strength, the unity they'd forged through hardship, their unspoken commitment to the future.

"Let's get this rocket finished," Dev said, his voice cracking before he cleared his throat. "Our astronaut needs to get to space."

"Mission control is ready for launch!" Cam declared as he snapped the last brick into place with a gratifying click. "The rocket's ready for liftoff!"

The pride in Val's gaze mirrored his son's as he checked out their handiwork. "Wow, buddy. That is one impressive piece of engineering."

"It's not just a model, you know," Dev chimed in, leaning back on his palms. "It's a symbol of what humans can achieve when they come together, work together."

"Like us?" Cam asked, his gaze flitting between the two men.

"Exactly like us," Dev confirmed, emotion swelling inside him and stealing his voice.

"Then we should capture this achievement," Val suggested, grabbing his phone off the side table. "Let's take a picture. A family photo with our Artemis."

Cam's face lit up brighter than any launchpad flare. "Can we put it next to the one with Mom and me after my first build?"

"Of course," Val replied as Dev moved into position behind the model, along with Cam. "I think that's the perfect place to hang it."

"All right, space explorers," Val announced, holding the phone at arm's length as he crowded in behind Dev and Cam to take the selfie. "Squeeze in close."

They huddled around the spacecraft, shoulder to shoulder, and Dev realized this picture would be more than just an image: it would be a keepsake of this very instant when everything seemed possible.

"Smile," Val said. "Everyone say 'Artemis!'"

Afterward, Val showed them the photo, his blue gaze locked on Dev's. "Perfect."

Dev nodded, knowing it was true.

* * * * *

If you enjoyed this story,
check out these other great reads from
Traci Douglass

Family of Three Under the Tree
Her Forbidden Firefighter
An ER Nurse to Redeem Him
Home Alone with the Children's Doctor

All available now!

HARLEQUIN
Reader Service

Enjoyed your book?

Try the perfect subscription for Romance readers and get more great books like this delivered right to your door.

See why over 10+ million readers have tried Harlequin Reader Service.

Start with a Free Welcome Collection with free books and a gift—valued over $20.

Choose any series in print or ebook.
See website for details and order today:

TryReaderService.com/subscriptions